W9-DCN-515

"As Larson explores the psychological torment of the young minister, he vividly captures the tension between the rigid confining atmosphere of the Puritan community and the freedom and natural exuberance of the new land."
Library Journal

"It's an enticing prospect: retelling a classic story from a new point of view. Charles Larson puts new souls in familiar bodies. His Hester is strong, strange, passionate and determined...Chillingworth a fascinating charlatan...Dimmesdale a mirror image of the original, reflected in the cracked eyeglasses of the minister. Larson circles the darker well of Hawthorne's tale, peering in and taking dips in the older writer's 19th century literary style."
The Detroit News

"The novel brilliantly re-creates the oppression of Puritanism as it crushes one sensitive soul."
World Literature Today

CHARLES R. LARSON, Professor of Literature at American University, is the author of two earlier novels and three volumes of literary criticism.

ARTHUR DIMMESDALE
CHARLES R. LARSON

 A BARD BOOK/PUBLISHED BY AVON BOOKS

AVON BOOKS
A division of
The Hearst Corporation
1790 Broadway
New York, New York 10019

The A & W Publishers, Inc. edition contains the follow-
ing Library of Congress Cataloging in Publication Data:
  Larson, Charles R.
Arthur Dimmesdale.

  I. Hawthorne, Nathaniel, 1804-1864. Scarlet letter.
1982 II. Title.
PS3562.A752A88   1982   813'.54   82-11587

First Bard Printing, February, 1984

For Roberta,
My Constant Muse

Chapter One

ARTHUR opened the door to his study, hastening past the women in the nave who were finishing their ministrations for early evening prayers, kerchief over his mouth, feigning a cold in case one of the busybodies tried to divert him from his objective. He coughed once or twice to simulate illness, wiped his nose, and walking through the narthex, left the security of First Church for the cacophony of the street, warmer air on this autumnal day immediately blowing against the folds of his cassock, whisking them like so many dead leaves. Trembling as much from the contrast with the air and the bright light as the recent event, he glanced at the house across the street where the Reverend John Wilson's wife was busy giving instructions to the gardener, then twisted abruptly to the right avoiding any exchange of greetings, and hurried past Market Place, handkerchief still over the lower extremities of his face, before anyone in the sparsely populated stalls could acknowledge his flight.

Reaching the end of the market, he turned left on High Street and increased his pace so that no dreary soul would accost him or request the comfort and solace of which his own broken body had need. Then he quickened his tread even more rapidly while holding his breath and counting his footsteps—a habit he had perfected down through the years to prohibit thinking: 184 steps to the twist in the road, past the entrance to the spring that fed Shelter Creek, past isolated houses, until he reached Milk Street where he turned once again to the left, the *idée fixe* in his mind changing from numbers to Hester, Hester, Hester, Hester Prynne. Then he relaxed his speed and replaced the handkerchief in one of the inner pockets of his robe, since no one was about on Milk Street this late afternoon in September, the first day of the equinox.

Shortly the fields of Elder Hardwick's farmlands gave way to woodland that led to the marsh, tall stately birch, maple, hemlock, and larch—the former tinted from the cool fall evenings, ablaze with isolated splotches of yellow and gold. As Arthur left the fields for the forest, he felt the slightest shiver cascade down his spine, of some vague undetermined nature, relief that he was about to return to the cocoon they had ravaged in the wood—away from the enjambment of the streets of Boston and the visibility of the bright day, away from his earlier fears of the forest, primeval haven of the dark unknown: Indians, witches, the great death.

"I am going to have your child," Hester had informed him minutes earlier, before Deacon Goodbody had rapped on the door of his study, interrupting Arthur's first moments of astonishment and horror.

"Are you certain?" he had managed to reply, turning white in his cassock, his greatest fear a reality instead of a possibility.

"Yes, I am certain," Hester replied, her face quite emotionless, as he had remembered it when she had arrived at the parish the year before after enduring an ill-fated voyage from the old country.

"I feared for this," Arthur had added, repeating himself before he continued: "I feared for this from the beginning—the blackest scourge of men's lives, the curse of the heathen and the lowly. It has leveled us to the common lot. I feared it like the night, Hester."

"I welcome it like the dawn," Hester replied, "and would not change what we have done should Hell itself open up before me and pull me into its flames." And then Deacon Goodbody had tapped on the door while Arthur had stood there, watching the hinged edifice move forward ever so slowly as the old gentleman had entered the study quite unexpectedly.

There was an ugglesome moment when Arthur—struck dumb by the interruption—had turned toward the elder and Hester had rustled through the door, her farewell no more than a whisper, more imagined than overheard by Arthur Dimmesdale on this fine autumn afternoon in 1641.

After a moment of feigned interest, Arthur had excused himself from the blundering elder and followed Hester through the aisle, into the church where the sisters of mercy were completing their work. But Hester had disappeared before he could determine what course or pathway his weary legs should take him or where or when their tracks would ever meet again: in his study, whose threshhold she had never crossed until this day, though he had been her spiritual confessor these many months since her arrival; in her own rooms, where she had long since given up waiting for her aged husband, feared lost at sea; or at their elfin grot in the forest, near Winthrop's Marsh, on an isle where they had met no more than three hurried times in the same number of months—an island, he knew, where they would no longer find any respite.

Arthur completed the dialogue in his mind, taking a stronger position than he had been able to assume in her presence:

"Hester, the penalty for adultery in Boston is death, have you forgotten? We will need to fly quickly away."

"You have nothing to fear, Arthur, since no one will ever know whom I have lain with."

"Then you must go away alone and give the child a proper name—something you can never do here, where even from a benevolent council the least you can expect is to be striped and scorned."

"You will be there, Arthur, to speak out for my salvation, whether death, bodily punishment, or public censure. They dare not go against your advice."

"I fear my inability to stand there defending you when I know that I am the one who should be standing in your stead."

"But you will do so, Arthur."

"But even at the very least, you will be branded with the letter *A* from a hot iron, like a common criminal, or forced to wear the crimson initial on your garment as long as you shall remain in this country, left to endure public embarrassment and ridicule."

"That I can endure as long as I know that your secrecy is assured. You have everything to lose. I have nothing."

"Oh, that we had never met in the forest on that fateful day."

"That, Arthur, I would never want to annul. It has given me a reason for existence far greater than you will ever know; it has lifted me out of the horror of the past."

"But there will be imprisonment also, Hester, once your condition is recognized by the villagers, followed by confinement for months after the child's birth—if it should live."

"She shall live."

And then Deacon Goodbody had entered Arthur's study and interrupted them in their discourse.

* * *

Arthur pulled up his cassock and ran through the forest, branches from larch and hemlock scratching out at his body, forcing him to trip over short, tussocky dry grasses and the loose clumps of earth formed by the late summer drought. They nearly canceled his quickened pace. The sun, high above and behind him, vanishing and then reappearing, shot forth blades of intense blindness, sharp as the edge of a scalpel—threatening to thwart his attempts to hide away. Avatars of white light mingled with the calls from chickadees and phoebes which came in autumn to feed on the red berries of the heart-shaped mayflowers, darkened and dried by the barrenness of the earth. The soil underneath him, formed from a carpet of leaves and needles, cushioned his erratic strides as he plunged deeper and deeper into the forest, to the verge of the marsh, bordered by the brook almost silenced by the summer's end.

Holding his breath, Arthur entered the grotto in the trees they had shaped for their secret meetings, then stood motionless for a minute, stifling his own erratic breathing, and listened for the identity of any foreign sound. All he could hear were the palpitations of his own heart.

After a minute, he collapsed on the ground, released a breath of stagnant air from his lungs, breathing fitfully through his mouth like some wild animal under hot pursuit. Fine drops of perspiration were breaking out all over his body from the hurried flight through the streets and the forest, his body soon drenched as though it had been immersed in a baptismal font. He pulled up his cassock and loosened the strings of his shoes, then took them off along with his damp stockings, his bare feet exposed like the translucent skin of a plucked chicken. The blue veins protruded as if they were about to explode. Quickly he glanced away from the naked white skin which reminded him of the weaknesses of the flesh. He contemplated soaking his feet in what was left of the brook, but was too exhausted to leave the security of the brush. Outside the shelter of their forest haven there was another world: foreboding even in the daylight.

Then fear overtook him as the forest which had seemed so quiet moments before tuned itself up like an orchestra about to undertake the performance of some dirge or morbid piece of music: insects and birds, the remaining water in the brook, the movement of the trees rushing in on him, threatening to bury him in a plethora of noises—his hearing, always sensitive, smothered in a barrage of undertones. The discord reminded him of a violin played out of tune and for a moment he contemplated covering his ears. He wondered if anyone had witnessed his flight through the woods? Had anyone followed him in his course of confusion? Were there unfriendly spirits surrounding him, waiting to pull him toward the porches of Hell? He squinted through his glasses, attempting to look through the wall of thick shrubbery.

Fear and self-loathing locked in combat within him. The body he hated, its white skin a reminder of his former purity, fear of the future and the unknown. Fear of discovery of his crime once Hester's condition became common knowledge. Fear of life's tenuous existence, and worse—fear of death. Death and fornication. Fornication that brought death, as the wise men had written.

"I am going to have your child, Arthur," Hester had revealed to him, her face unable to conceal the slightest hint of perversity, the merest suggestion of intentionality. "You will be exposed for what you are—a hypocrite."

Had Hester been in league with the Devil? Sent as his minion to tempt him? To bring about his assured downfall? Was she really a married woman who had lost her husband at sea, or a common hussy cleverly planted to bring about his demise? Whom could he trust? Whom could he tell? Anyone? Was this what Hester's condition could bring about so quickly—distrust of the one person he had ever loved, the only person with whom he could speak?

"We will burn in Hell, Hester. We will be branded, flogged, and sentenced to death as the mere mortals that we are."

"Not you, Arthur. Only me. Your future is secure. Though I will wear the scarlet letter on my bosom, you will bear the deeper mark of our transgression. The strength you have given me these many months will guide you in our future—until the day when we are free to marry."

"Suppose the child dies, Hester, or you miscarry before the public record is known? There are still those possibilities. Perhaps not everything has been lost."

"Never! The child is mine forever." And then Deacon Goodbody had entered Arthur's study and Hester had vanished like one of Mistress Hibbins's spirits of the dark.

Arthur closed his eyes and listened to the woods about him, mingled with sounds of Hester in childbirth, crying out his name, revealing the identity of the child's father to the midwives who attended her. Worse, as he lay there on the mossy carpet he imagined the infant, an image of his own identity—immediately revealing to any passerby the paternity that could never be kept in hiding. The child, a deformed monster, yet with Arthur's features, pointing a hand with six stubby fingers at the assistant pastor of First Church. The child at baptism, locking its arms around its father like a vise, refusing to let him go. The child which Arthur knew, dared even wish, had an equal chance of premature death.

"The *A*, Hester, they have sentenced you to wear the *A* for perpetuity," Arthur told her, the verdict of the council revealed. "It bodes no good; it will burn you like a blaze from Hell."

"It will not matter. There is nothing that can take away what we have done. We stand transfigured by our past, our future, and our love."

"But we will not be able to meet again until all of this is past. For months, even years, Hester. What good is a life like that? The *A* has altered our past as much as our future." And then Deacon Goodbody had opened the door to Arthur's study and brought with him all of the fears of the outside world.

Arthur opened his eyes and listened, the drumming in his ears unceasing. Here, in the midst of the forest, in what should have been the quietest strictures of his narrowing world, even here there was noise and penetration from the outside—the birds, the trees, the water, and the insects; the expected chorus of exterior sounds. But worse, when he listened carefully, he could hear faintly, as though muffled by wool, the steady falling of an axe coming from the distance. Someone—far away but still near enough that it could be heard—was chopping down a tree, forging a path through the forest that mingled with the jungle in his mind. Someone was entering this sealed-off universe Arthur had thought was safe and protected from the outside evils.

Focusing his eyes more immediately upon the short trees that surrounded him, he discovered that even here where the sun rarely shone directly, the leaves on the maple and birch trees were beginning to change, to alter according to nature's annual cycle. Many of the brighter leaves had already fallen to the ground where shortly they would crumble into the compost that rejuvenated the very trees from which they had fallen, the leaves which symbolized their yearly death. As he watched another leaf flutter to the earth, Arthur realized that here also, in this isolated grotto, time had discovered no hiding place. In a month or two, even less, the maples and birches would have shed their ragged blankets, leaving only the gymnospermous trees to conceal them. And they would offer little protection at all. Had this event not changed their lives, their activities would have moved out of the safety of the unseen and into the realm of the visible. Where would they have met after all the leaves had fallen? Where would they have met in the dead of winter? The cocoon had already been on the verge of disintegrating before their eyes, and they had been unable to recognize its harbingers.

The *A*. The *A* that Hester would be assigned for adultery, as the mark of an adulteress. Arthur thought about the symbol, feared it too, the simple acrostic that Hester would wear on her bosom, announcing to all of the world her allegorical life. The *A* that would set her off from those around her forever more. What would it augur for her future?

Affliction?

Amaurosis?

Alone, aside, apart, asunder? All these and more as her already ascertained future.

Anguish? Yes, and anxiety mingled with alienation?

Accouchement or amblosis? He was afraid to ask.

Affection, ardor, amorino? Their amour? Their arousal? Their awe?

Adam and the apple this new-world Eve had used to astonish him from his former ways?

Agenbite of inwit about their allogamous affair?

Anathema and apartness for Hester in what would certainly be a new-found anonymity?

Anomie and anxiety about this albatross, this allonym?

Agony, ashame, and atonement for their assignation?

Atheism for which there was no antidote?

Angel, apostle, apotheosis?

No, the *A*, he knew, would have only one meaning for the angry eyes that would focus upon it: Arthur.

Arthur Dimmesdale.

Chapter Two

RISING into the air, further and further up into the sky, Arthur hallucinating on his bed, inched his way to the edge and looked downward: back at the earth, hundreds of feet below him. The bed kept rising, moving still further away from the land below him, supported on a gigantic pillar, rising higher into the sky. What would prevent him from falling off and trembling back to the ground? What would keep the bed suspended there safely, high above the masses of people he could identify like tiny specks of offal? Alternately, Arthur was petrified at the fear of falling from this moving obelisk and elated at the physical thrill of soaring so rapidly through the air away from the earth. Fear and freedom juxtaposed as Arthur floated alone above the earth with no one to protect him or chastise him for flying away.

The movement increased, the bed moving like a kite through the heavens, so quickly that Arthur held his breath—feared, again, that he would fall, down to the earth where his body would be broken into a thousand tiny pieces. Then, with a final thrust through the firmament, the propulsion concluded, and Arthur found himself—for the third time in as many weeks—lying on his bed in the midst of the council: Governor Bellingham, the Reverend John Wilson, the community of elders.

"She should be forced to reveal the renegade's identity," Governor Bellingham imparted, his voice establishing the harsh reality of the tribunal. "If she refuses after the period of her confinement, she should be publicly flogged."

"The child should know its father," a bearded man in steepled hat replied.

14

"Bring out the punitive apparatus," Governor Bellingham continued, "so that we may make our decision."

Arthur, aware that he was strapped into his bed and a prisoner in their midst, turned his head as the doors of the chamber burst open and three men, dressed solely in black, carried in the equipment: bilboes, pillories, stocks, and ducking stools, their movements slow and suggestive, like a dance of death.

"She should be burned at the stake like a witch!" one of the elders shrieked out to the others, his skin the color of a shriveled lemon.

"Have mercy!" Reverend John Wilson replied, his voice a mere wisp of air. "She has suffered enough for her transgressions."

"But her accomplice still walks among us free like the deer in the forest," Governor Bellingham replied, glancing suggestively at Arthur tied to his bed. "Tell her that she will not be punished if she reveals his identity—otherwise she will be tortured."

"The *A* is sufficient," Reverend Wilson responded, his voice a mere whisper compared to the stridency of the governor's. "The *A* is enough."

"Yea, if it be branded on her forehead," another elder interjected, "where it will burn into her brain and remind her of her passion."

"Mercy, mercy. Have compassion for this pitiful creature," Reverend Wilson repeated. "If it be the *A* that she must wear, let it be sewn on her garment and worn as long as she remain amongst us. The child alone will be the constant reminder of her sin."

"And if the child should die, then she will be free of any such memory," another leader interjected with surprising force.

"We need not worry ourselves about that until we see," Reverend Wilson whispered, his voice so faint that Arthur wondered if anyone had heard his suggestion.

"This action is not sufficient, I fear," another centurian continued, "to curtail the lust of this cunning vixen. Her lover must be known. At the very least, there must be a branding of two letters, *A* and *D*."

A.D.—Arthur Dimmesdale. Arthur felt moisture break out upon him, fever covering his body as if someone had thrown a bucket of water upon him in his bed. *AD, AD, AD.* By that his transgressions would be known. By those initials his identity announced to the world.

"No, it must not be. The *A* is sufficient—"

Then there was a loud rapping on the window of his bedroom

chamber, bringing him back to the earth and the messenger from Master Brackett, the jailer, announcing the time of Hester's delivery. "Her time has arrived. You are awaited, sir." And when Arthur did not reply, "Are you awake?" followed by another rapping.

"I will be there directly," Arthur muttered in confused reply. He sat up in the bed that he now realized was resting securely on the floor.

AD, AD, AD. What if it had been the council's decision that Hester should wear the more traditional markings of an adulteress, *AD*, his own initials? He placed the palms of his hands flat on the four-poster in order to make certain it was securely planted on the floor. "I will be there soon," he replied, though the messenger had long since left.

Arthur reached for his glasses from the nightstand and slipped them over his nose, throwing the covers aside and climbing out of bed, his body under the rough woolen blankets drenched in perspiration. It was early in the month of March and outside the temperature was nearly zero, the winter ice and snow heaped high like the refuse piles in some arctic kingdom. In the darkness, he crossed the floor to the table, located the flintlock, and, after striking it several times, lit a tallow candle. The room was brought into subdued illumination; outside there was nothing but darkness, and a glance at the clock informed him that there were several hours before dawn. He wanted to wash the perspiration away from his torso, but the water in the basin was frozen solid, and Arthur knew there was no time to prepare even a hurried toilet.

Quickly, he wiped himself with a faded blue cloth, pulled on his woolen undergarments before covering them with his winter cassock, his breath visible in the cold air of the room. Although the coals in the fireplace had burned out, Arthur did not feel the chill's discomfort. Already he knew that his fever would soon revert from heat to cold, and the walk outside to the prison would do him no good.

He pulled on his boots, then his coat and gloves, and—after lighting the lantern with the candle—opened the door to his room, the light under the Widow Finney's door revealing her own state of arousal. In the sitting room, the coals of the larger fireplace were still sending forth a hot, cold whiteness. Arthur crossed the room, released the bolt in the front door, and felt the bitter cold blast him on his unshaven face.

The sky was clear above him, a crisp deep azure, sprinkled with recognizable specks, though there was no moon. As he trudged through the piles of snow and ice—a delicate balancing act in the darkness with the lamp as his only illumination—his body began to contort, to shift from heat, through shiver, to cold, as Arthur's mind in turn let loose the barrage of fears that had been swelling up inside him ever since that September day when Hester informed him of her altered state. Would the child look like him, confess to all of Boston its secret paternity? Would Hester—nay, *had* Hester—already divulged his identity, cried out in pain for him in her childbirth and revealed to the attendant midwives his complicity in their act? Would he reach the prison and be greeted by their knowing faces?

He trembled at the thought of it, the weight of his winter clothing suddenly quite overbearing. Though they had met only once alone together since September—when Master Brackett had slipped out of her cell for a few minutes—Hester had quickly requested that he be present at her delivery, in case she called out his name uncontrollably. Was it already too late to keep their secret to themselves alone? What did it mean that Hester was already in her labor, since the child had not been expected until the end of the month—two or three weeks later? Would it be stillborn, a monster, a devil? For the thousandth time Arthur wanted to fly away, run away from Boston alone and leave Hester to her ill-chosen state, but now—in the winter's dark remorse—there was no escape route. Like most people of his time, he feared the unseen world around him, the dark shadows that grasped toward him. If the choice were his alone, he would never venture out into the world of nighttide.

It was but a short walk from Arthur's lodgings to the Boston prison, normally six minutes' duration, but on this icy night, Arthur wondered if he hadn't entered some polar region on the outbanks of Hell—the cold, bitter air from the sea, so harsh it threatened to burn his flesh with the intensity of white heat. Though there had been no new accumulation of precipitation during the day, the streets—as they had been for weeks on end—were covered in an avalanche of crusty snow, piled high by conscientious denizens who had tried to keep the footpaths open between buildings. The world everywhere was covered in a blanket of whiteness, and the stillness of the crystalline obscurity frightened Arthur to no small degree as he trudged through the footways, his lantern held high in one hand so that it would not knock against any of the piles of snow and ice.

As he walked closer to Market Place and the prison, he started to cough. The catarrh in his chest began to agitate his throat, causing him to cough uncontrollably, and he stopped for a minute listening to his sounds echo through the empty market, the stalls closed for the winter. The muscles in his throat contracted more rhythmically as Arthur coughed, unable to stop the rasping noise exploding from his throat. The outside air continued to burn into his flesh: through his nose, his throat, and down into his lungs, a chain of reactions as each section of his respiratory system felt as if it were on fire. Arthur stood in the cold darkness, his body rigid, anger and rage rushing out of him as the cough finally subsided deep within his chest, like some rare strain of malignancy, waiting for the moment when it would erupt again. Yet he was relieved, for he did not want to reach the prison in this afflicted state. Rather, he had hoped for a calmness and serenity to transform his body into the state of quiescence he had been longing for for many months. Perhaps the birth of the child would bring with it peace and quietude instead of these renewed feelings of fear and self-hatred.

He covered his mouth with his left glove as if he could wipe away the coughs and throw them away like so many broken icicles. And then, as he was about to place his hand on the prison door and turn the handle, he identified Hester's painful screams, penetrating the heavy wooden edifice and the cold, exterior world. He thought her shriek might drive him mad. Should he turn around and run away, or twist the handle of the door? Then to his wonder, Arthur felt his body twitch, as if his system had shifted over to some new source of energy; he turned the knob and entered the Boston prison.

The draught of hot, humid air from inside the building almost knocked him over—the heat from the fireplace, the moisture from the boiling water, the smell of blood. As soon as he closed the door behind him, he was immediately blinded by the combination of forces acting upon his spectacles. They were drenched in a layer of moisture from the contrast with the outside air and instantly clouded over. He could see nothing, only hear voices—including one he assumed was Hester's. With the awkwardness of his gloved hands, he grasped for his glasses, removing them from his face, momentarily hearing a sharp, high ping, but there was little improvement: his myopia from years of diligent study reducing him at such times to a child in need of guidance and care. The space around him (the entryroom to the small three-celled prison) was reduced to a spectrum of discontinuous colors and shapes.

"The child is coming now," someone informed him—some male voice he thought he recognized but could not identify. As it had been earlier while he was still in bed, Arthur felt as if he were drenched in perspiration, his body electrified, as if *he* were the one giving birth. He uttered a singular cough, pulled off his gloves, then grasped his empty hand at his coat and tried to remove it, aware that someone was trying to assist him.

It was Master Brackett. "She has been calling for you, sir," the jailer informed him, placing the heavy garment somewhere beyond Arthur's ken.

He tried to focus his eyes upon the blurry figure in front of him, then rubbed his glasses on his woolen cassock in an attempt to clean them, but as soon as he placed them back on his nose, they were smeared with moisture. He removed them a second time and held them close to his face, noticing that one of the lenses had cracked, the differences between the inside and the outdoor temperatures being so great that one lens had been unable to withstand the shock.

He held his glasses several inches away from his face so that he could glance about the room. The obscured shapes and colors began to take on a new identity: the movement of the women, especially, came partially into focus. One of them was standing over the steaming kettle at the fireplace, stirring the white woolen cloths with a large wooden ladle. Another was building up the fire from a stack of nearby wood. And then there was Master Brackett, sitting rigidly in a chair, looking as if he had been overthrown from his usual domain. Hester, he knew, was in one of the cells, from where he could hear voices emanating.

"Should I go in and see her?" Arthur asked no one in particular, rubbing his glasses steadily on his cassock, as if he could wipe the crack away.

"Wait and I will see," the woman who had been kindling the fire answered, walking into one of the other rooms.

"I could hear her cries outside the building," Arthur mumbled to the woman who was boiling the pieces of cloth. "Has she long to go?"

"You are mistaken, Reverend Dimmesdale," the woman replied. "She has made no noise since the contractions began. She has uttered no sound at all."

Confused, Arthur glanced at Master Brackett, wondering what he had meant by the statement that Hester had been asking for him, but the jailer, who seemed to be in a world of his own, looked at him as though no explanation were necessary for this inconsistency in their dialogue.

"Will it be long?" Arthur asked the woman at the fire, one of the gossips in his parish for whom he felt no special affection. He continued rubbing his glasses, since they remained covered with moisture.

"Hours maybe," the woman replied, looking at him as if he had no right to be in attendance here, though Arthur had been present at the delivery of many of Boston's younger citizens. "Perhaps less. It is difficult to tell with the first one. Her water has not yet broken. You might as well sit down and try to get some rest, since I fear that Master Brackett has called you here for naught." She gave a contemptuous glance at the jailer, who tried to withdraw even further into his chair.

Arthur stood perplexed, holding the glasses away from his face so that he could focus part of the room before him, waiting for something to happen. Then the woman who had been building up the fire returned from Hester's cell and told him, "She has requested that you do not enter her room, since she fears you are unaccustomed to such matters," and once again Arthur pondered the inconsistency of these remarks. What had he heard screaming outside? Why did Master Brackett say that Hester had asked for him? Why did Hester refuse to let him see her?

Later—hours later, Arthur guessed—his nerves frayed from the overcharged atmosphere and no change in Hester's condition, he decided to leave the prison for the calmness of his study at First Church at the other end of the market. He would still be close to the prison if his presence were needed, and he could escape the excessive heat of the delivery room. Arthur felt as if he had been swimming around inside a sac of amniotic fluid; the heat was so stultifying he had been unable to rest, and his glasses still fogged up whenever he placed them on his nose.

He requested his winter coat from Master Brackett, said his farewells to the midwives, and left the prison, informing them of his proximity at the church should he be needed. "Tell Hester Prynne that I will come if she asks for me." Then he braced himself for the cold winter air, immediately aware of the vivid contrast once he closed the door behind him.

Once outside, he was able to see again. On this bitter March morning, the market was empty except for one lone shadow at the other end of the square. Specter or substance, he could not be certain. All he could see were the head and shoulders, the lower portion of the chimera hidden by the piles of snow. The sky was a robin's-egg blue, though it was still quite dark. Arthur watched the mysterious figure disappear behind a wall, and then he trudged through the snowy and slippery pathways to First Church, coughing once or twice, aware when he reached the edifice that he had left his lantern at the prison.

He entered First Church by the door at the back behind the altar, shook his clothing, and reflexively muttered a prayer—as he always did when he entered the House of God. There was no problem with his glasses this time—the church was as cold as his own bedroom chamber during the night—though he had been conscious of the cracked lens ever since he placed the glasses back on his face. At this early hour of the morning, no one else was in the building. He walked to the security of his study, free of the need to chatter with John Wilson or any of his parishioners who would later frequent the church for silent matins.

In his office, he removed his winter coat and hung it upon a wooden peg at the back of the door he had carefully closed behind him. Then he sighed and sat down in the chair behind his desk, wondering if he would be able to sleep in such an uncomfortable position.

He was awakened somewhat later by the screams from Hester's pain—so he momentarily thought, determined that he had not been dreaming—Hester's cries cutting through the silences of the cold, winter morn. They were part of no dream, for he was awake, and saliva had run from the corner of his mouth, down his chin, and onto his cassock. He wiped the drool away with his hand and heard the voice again—so sharp and piercing he thought it might shatter the stained-glass windows above the altar in the sanctuary. But when he jumped up from his chair, the screaming stopped.

He was cold, nay, he was freezing, the temperature of his body lowered by his sleep. He rubbed his hands together, tried to warm them, tried to restore their faulty circulation. Then he moved about his study vigorously in an attempt to increase the circulation in his entire body, but he quickly grew tired of the exercise and returned to his chair where he fell back into a deep slumber.

The ballet of women around him—slow, protective, reassuring—prepared him for the horrors of the descent. When the contractions began and his cervix began to dilate, he took comfort from their proximity and for a time even managed to ignore the threatening pain. But then, later, he realized that there was no way to obviate the increasing menace attacking his body. When he screamed, the women assisting him held his arms and the upper portion of his torso, pulled against him in the opposite direction with such force that Arthur felt that his limbs might be wrenched from his body. Were they there to assist or destroy him? His bowels evacuated reflexively, the foul odor of feces mixed with the less offensive smells of blood and alcohol, as the opening between his legs rapidly contracted. Steam was coming up from the heap of hot cloths near his body, and someone was wiping off the drops of perspiration that had formed on his brow. The contractions, which momentarily slowed down, increased with new intensity. Though he had been determined to hide his pain and above all to keep Hester's identity a secret—he screamed unconstrainedly, cursing his Maker and then Hester for the predicament she had brought upon him—swore that if he lived through the delivery he would hate the child and Hester forever. The midwives looked at him with their knowing glances, one of them mumbling something about Mistress Prynne that he was not able to understand.

The heat in the delivery room increased, the oozing from every pore and orifice in his body had become so overpowering that Arthur felt as if he were drowning in the liquid excesses of his own filthy body: blood, excrement, urine, drool, and sweat. He believed he was walking through the fires of Hell, flamed by his own bodily excrescences. His skin was bloated, stretched so tightly, the hole in the middle of his body which he could feel but not see felt as if someone had thrust a slippery foreign object into his abdomen and were moving it hysterically in and out. The midwives had turned a sickening color of green, and one of them, he could see, had sprouted a hairy tail, poking out of the back of her blood-smeared garments.

The pain he knew would never cease but would last forever, pulling at his insides, unraveling all of his internal organs, the slippery rope coming out yard after yard after yard. Though the salt in the corners of his eyes made it impossible to see, he could feel all of the intensity and the pressure as one of the women pulled the final section of his innards away from his body, yanked it out in front of him, wrenching the cord of his being so violently that he knew he had lost forever the tumor that had polluted his body for so many months. Then, with a suddenness and brutality that shocked him, his legs fell back upon the bed, aching; his heart stopped beating; his breathing also curtailed, as the foreign object shot forth from the opening between his legs and the gaping hole began to retract into its former shape. He heard the child cry out, and felt a refreshing dew annoint his body, bringing with it a state of passivity he knew he would always remember.

Arthur slept.

When he was awakened by the screams, he was terrified at the sudden thought that Hester had died in childbirth. His stomach muscles were contracting, Hester's screams were so piercing that he had to cover his ears, and he was conscious of the smell of blood. When he jumped from his chair, the screaming stopped, one long painful peal assuring him that Hester was dead. The idea was so terrifying that it took him several minutes to collect his senses and realize what, in fact, had actually happened. He had lost his glasses, and when he tried to pull on his boots, he realized that his face and hand and much of his clothing were covered in blood.

"My Lord, my Lord, my Lord," he mumbled repeatedly, groping on the floor for his spectacles, his boots—anything that would explain what had happened.

Then he found his glasses—or, more accurately, what was left of them, for the cracked lens was missing from the misshapen wire frames. He jerked his hands up to his face, forcing the frames over his nose and his ears and his focus sharpened considerably —enough so that he could examine his hands.

The tip of the thumb of his right hand had been sliced so deeply that the blood that oozed from its fissure looked as if it were flowing from a hidden spring at the end of the digit. When he pushed the flap of loose skin back together with his right index finger, Arthur comprehended what had happened. It was only a matter of locating the broken lens, somewhere, he knew, on the floor; but first he had to staunch the flow of blood, since it was apparent from the scarlet that covered the front of his cassock that he had been bleeding for some time.

His finger burned with a sharp pain, and when he took a step toward the door of his study, he heard his foot crush part of the lens that had fallen from his glasses. He flung open the door of his office, expecting to see someone in the nave of the church, but was relieved that no one was there. Then he walked to the back entrance, opened the outer door, and walked out into the snow-filled courtyard where he bathed his injured thumb in the cold, white snow. The brisk morning air jolted his body, sending shock waves through his entire figure, but—more importantly—awakening him, bringing him back to the world of the living. He was surprised that there was still no one to be seen in the street or in the market, and he wondered if his mind had been playing tricks with the time.

When the accidental bloodletting finally stopped, he was surprised by the great loss of fluid he had suffered: the pile of snow he had used to curtail the bleeding had turned a sickening crimson, and he could see a trail of bright, cerise drops in the snow, running back to the door of First Church. Arthur sucked in a draught of cold air and walked back to the door, through the church, and into his study where he wrapped a clean handkerchief around his injured thumb. Then, feeling slightly faint, exhausted from his sympathetic labor, he returned to his chair, looking at the blood that still surrounded him, spattering his clothing, the floor, even his boots. After a minute, he spotted the broken and crushed lens from his glasses—half of it still intact, the other half shattered into a dozen pieces by his boots.

Then there was a hesitant tap on the door of his study, followed by Master Brackett's question: "Are you there, sir? The baby has been born—alive."

"I'll be there in a minute," Arthur replied through the closed door.

"Are you all right, sir?" the jailer questioned, his query prompted, Arthur knew, by the drops of blood leading from the door.

"Yes, I'm all right. I'll be there in a minute. What time is it?"

"About six-thirty, sir."

As Arthur draped his winter coat over his shoulders, careful to avoid any pressure on his right thumb, he heard the jailer's reluctant footsteps disappearing in the distance. Moments later when he left the narthex, he braced himself for the bitter cold that he knew would be followed by the tropical intensity of Hester's delivery room. Then, to his surprise, he realized that he had forgotten to ask whether his child was male or female.

Chapter Three

THE child was given the name Pearl by her mother, without the benefit of consultation with Arthur Dimmesdale. The Reverend John Wilson informed his assistant pastor of this choice three days after the child's birth, during which time Arthur had held no private conversation with his mistress.

If the truth be known, Arthur had spent most of the hours of those days confined to his bed in the room he rented from the Widow Finney, the cough he had harbored for several weeks lashing out with renewed fury. Arthur was not, however, the only citizen of Boston detained in his rooms during that period of time, for the snowstorm that ravaged the community the day of Hester's delivery brought with it such havoc that most of the citizens became prisoners in their own households. Arthur, however, was twice cursed: by the storm and by his weakened body, shaken by a near ungovernable fear and cough—the first of many illnesses that he would suffer (often with no visible cause or cure) for the remainder of his days.

When John Wilson visited Arthur Dimmesdale on the third day after Hester's delivery and informed him of the child's name, Arthur had immediately begun coughing, discovering in the midst of his attack that his bodily affliction could serve as a protective covering, camouflaging the deeper, emotional lesions that troubled his soul.

"The child has been given the name Pearl," Reverend Wilson announced to him.

When there was no response from Arthur, Reverend Wilson continued, "It has been our decision in your absence, I am afraid, that both mother and child remain in confinement for three months to assure their health and comfort. At that time, Hester Prynne will stand on the scaffold for three hours, holding her child for all to see, and wearing the letter *A*, as you know, sewn upon her bosom. After that, she will be free to leave the confines of the prison.''

Arthur trembled in his bed, perspiration covering his brow. Then Reverend Wilson added, in his usual whispering voice, ''Methinks that she will never reveal the identity of her lover, and perhaps that is just as well, for he will certainly bear the deeper wound of his anonymity.''

When Arthur reflected upon the name given to their child, he was troubled by Hester's apparent mockery. Was this child, this Pearl, the irritant of their imperfection—the fatal flaw that had permitted him to remove himself so easily from their lives? Would Pearl grow up a demon child, a black Pearl—an outcast like some deformed lustrous concretion, so commonly discovered in oysters of the sea, or would her life be that of the perfectly rounded aureole, nature's rarity and perfection? Arthur tried not to think about such matters. Her name would bring no good, yet he himself had made no attempt to communicate with Hester during these troubled times.

Increasingly, during the ensuing months, Arthur took to his bed: in the late March snows and the April showers that followed, when the snow and ice piled high on the streets of Boston began to melt and run toward the sea, when spring broke forth through branches and spongy ground and the cycle of regeneration began its yearly flow. Arthur's cough gave way to fever, the periods of cold and dry passions bowing to sleepless nights, as he lay on his bed unable to escape the feelings of remorse that dominated his waking hours.

Hester, he knew, he had failed, left alone with the weight of their crime, the child a constant reminder of their sin. As the days turned into weeks and then months, Arthur wondered how he could ever correct this horrible mistake: leaving Hester alone, publicly to wear the mark of her transgression. How could Hester survive all of this public humiliation? How should he go about communicating with her? His mind was obsessed with meeting her, talking to her about the events that had transpired, but—though he wracked his mind for days on end—he knew that there was no possibility of visiting her without arousing suspicions. Nor was there any way that he could write to her and express his many troubled feelings without the fear of discovery and immediate recrimination. And

Hester, he feared, had surely come to hate him for his timidity as he had come to loathe himself.

"In Adam's fall, we sinned all"—the educational rhyme taught to schoolchildren—became a kind of obsession, entering and exiting his mind with a frequency that knew no control. In Adam's fall, we sinned all. He and Hester had sinned and were cursed, though he doubly because of the secrecy of his crime. Pearl, their child, likewise, the visible hieroglyph, the byproduct of their past, the scoria of their uncontrollable lusts.

When he attempted to consider the matter rationally, Arthur knew that the child—who should have bound them together—had become not only a living symbol of their crime but also an embodiment of all his fears of the future, the child who would one day look upon him and recognize in his face the markings of her own. Never before had he experienced such ambivalent feelings. Arthur dreaded the first encounter with mother and child, the second, even the third. He thought of Pearl and wept, both from fear and longing. What could he do to rectify the errors of the past? In Adam's fall, we sinned all . . .

He began to conceive of his body as a vessel of pollution and filth, though in truth this was a concept he had believed in all of his life, one he had been taught as a child and then instilled in others as an adult, ever since he had assumed the role of spiritual leader to the lost souls of this godforsaken land: death was the only conceivable punishment for sin; death was the greatest fear. It was a simple matter. He had sinned and he would die and by his death be denied everlasting life. He, Arthur Dimmesdale, a Visible Saint to his flock, was the most polluted of all of his parishioners, his life—and the death he would shortly encounter—a mockery of his faith. Sin brought death, and death was the greatest punishment God had sent his afflicted flock. Adam had ushered in death for all mankind; Arthur was only his disciple, duplicating his forebear's earlier sin. In Adam's fall, we sinned all, but Arthur had sinned more than others.

He considered the matter of Hester's punishment: wearing the scarlet A. By such action, Hester would be publicly ridiculed, but she would also, in time, be washed free of her sin. By the letter A she would be punished and liberated, released of her terrible encumbrance. Arthur thought of other recreants who had been similarly punished: thieves who had been branded with the letter T; forgers who had worn the letter F, branded on their foreheads; burglars who had had both ears cut off for their crimes, a visible warning for others not to trust them. Some years before he had arrived in New England, there was the story of a woman who for her adultery with an Indian had been forced to wear the figure of a Native sewn on her left arm, a clear indication of her intercourse with the Devil. After all, if the Indian, as one of God's unenlightened creatures, was in league with the Devil, then it followed that the Indian *was* the Devil. It was a matter of elementary logic, as was his own crime. By fornication, he had sinned; by sinning he had placed himself in league with the Devil; by familiarity with Satan, he had assigned himself to that certain death which was Hell. Unlike Hester—unlike all of the thieves and burglars who wore their markings visibly—he, Arthur Dimmesdale, whose sin was hidden away, would be tortured endlessly for the crime of concealment. How could he continue ministering to his flock without bringing contamination to them all? In Arthur's fall, we sinned all . . .

What could he do to wash away these sins that had polluted his body? Perhaps it was already too late. In a few more days, Hester would walk from the prison to the public scaffold in the marketplace and openly display the symbol of her humiliation, while he, the assistant pastor of First Church, holiest of the holy, would sit with the other dignitaries, the hidden canker slowly destroying his body.

His child had been given the name Pearl because Arthur had been unable to act.

Chapter Four

Hester's period of public humiliation arrived, the day Arthur feared as the beginning of his own concealed mortification. If he could live through the trial—if Hester kept her identity a secret and he could conceal his own inner tensions—he would have survived the three most difficult examinations: Hester's confession that she was with child, her delivery, her penitence on the scaffold.

During the night he had been unable to sleep except by fits and snatches, his mind dominating the physical need for rest and quietude. What if Hester blundered and accidentally revealed his identity, uncontrollably spitting out his name? What was to prevent her from collapsing under the sheer weight of public ignominy? How would she ever endure the public scorn of three hours exposure, standing on the scaffold with Pearl, her body tense from the unendurable need for stoicism? If some irate citizen shouted at her—or, worse, threw some foreign object—what would prevent her from collapsing on the scaffold and revealing his name? Were he in her stead, Arthur doubted if he could endure such humiliation without caving in. It was bad enough that he would have to be one of Hester's inquisitors, pleading with her to reveal the identity of her lover. Would he be able to endure the grand inquisition if their places were reversed? It was the height of folly to stand before her and demand that she reveal his identity as her lover. Was anyone more hypocritical than he? What if Hester had changed her mind?

In the months since her delivery, Arthur had discovered no secret way of communicating with Hester, no way of discussing their symbolic arcanum. On the few occasions when he had spoken to her, it had always been in the presence of John Wilson or other village leaders; and Hester had remained steadfast in her reply: "The father of my child concerns you not. That is my secret alone—and his." Then she would turn her back to them and attend to her child. Once when Pearl cried out in his presence, Arthur thought that he would faint and fall upon the floor, but no one noticed the swaying of his body, and Hester quieted the child before its crying forced him to yell out in reply. What would happen if she cried at him today?

In the morning, before the Widow Finney had awakened, Arthur slipped out of his bed, prepared a hasty toilet, and left the confines of the house for his morning constitutional. It was early in the month of June, and the cool breeze from the direction of the ocean and the clearness of the sky foretold a mild, summer day. Later in the afternoon, there would perhaps be a sufficient number of clouds to shade Hester from the direct rays of the sun, though at the moment the sky was clear except for a wisp of moisture in the direction of the sea.

Arthur walked at a brisk and determined pace in order that his appearance convey the impression of preoccupation, lest the members of his flock who encountered him be given any thoughts of interrupting him from his pious thoughts. It was impossible, of course, for anyone in his position to avoid the matter of communication, so he hastened a curt "good morning" with whomever he passed and then, quickly, avoided any further glance in their direction. Conversation thus thwarted, he was able to continue on his way.

With no set pattern for his walk, he was surprised at where his feet were leading him: toward Prison Lane and the place of Hester's confinement. Though he checked himself and turned down another pathway before he stood directly in front of the edifice, he marveled at the misanthropy of the colony's earliest settlers. The prison was one of the original structures of the community, its foreboding porticoes and ponderous door a warning of the failures of the covenant those hearty settlers had envisioned in the New World. Arthur wondered about the uncountable number of visits he had made to the miscreants who had temporarily resided within the confines of the deeply weathered structure.

He quickened his pace as if his proximity to the prison might contaminate him, though what troubled him more was the thought of Hester and Pearl incarcerated there and the possibility of hearing their voices inside, especially the child's wails. What could be more unnatural than beginning one's life inside a prison? What havoc would the experience wreak on the child when it became an adult? The streets were becoming populated with other villagers out for early morning errands, and he knew that if he did not return to his rooms quickly, it would be impossible to avoid any conversation about Hester Prynne's day of reckoning. She was, after all, the subject of everyone's gossip, since there could hardly be a soul in the community unaware that this was the day of her release from prison.

Approaching the edge of Market Square, by necessity—unless he chose to retrace his steps—he tried to restore his early morning demeanor. It was a little as if he wore a sign on his person: do not intrude upon my thoughts; do not trouble me during my walk. The market was already knotted with people at this early hour: sellers of fish and produce, surrounded by the refuse of their wares, housewives making purchases for the tables of their families; and here and there a horse-drawn cart, laden with other foods brought from the country and contributing to the oppressive odor of the area. Though there were few people he could not have recognized if he had so desired, Arthur assiduously avoided any contact with his countrymen. Moreover, at this time of the year, the market was a place to be avoided: mud from the recent spring rainstorms had mixed with animal offal, producing a greenish slime that was to be eluded at all possible cost.

Arthur was about to leave the edge of the market when he glanced in the direction of a tobacco seller and noticed two figures he had never observed before. The taller one was an Indian, certainly a common enough sight in Arthur's environs, especially on market days when the square often became populated with these unenlightened peoples bartering away their colorful handiwork. From the angle where Arthur was standing, it was difficult to tell the age of the figure: bare-chested except for the multiple strings of beads that adorned the upper regions of his torso, and long, braided hair dangling over his shoulders. The Indian appeared to be engaged in heated conversation with the tobacco seller.

The second figure was the more perplexing since he, too, gave the appearance of living in nature's wilds, though he was not a red man. Like the Indian's, this stranger's gray hair was long and unkempt, and, though unbraided, it reached the tops of his shoulders—one of which was clearly higher than the other—where it suggested that it had been chopped off with the aid of some primitive instrument. The figure also wore beads around his neck—

albeit only one strand like a choker—and though his faded shirt was clearly a product of European civilization, his breeches had been sewn from coarse leather, the kind trappers wore in the forest to protect their legs. All of these features were highlighted by the stranger's weathered skin—darkened almost to the hue of the Indian's—and a floppy hat perched upon his skull.

The image of the two outsiders that darkened Arthur's countenance had been created in his mind's eye in a manner of seconds while he paused fleetingly during his walk—midway, as it were, between two steps, though when he later considered the nature of the anomaly, Arthur felt as though he had stood there with one leg in the air for a considerably longer duration. At that moment, the hump-shouldered man turned nearly halfway around and glanced at Arthur, who was pushing off in the opposite direction.

The effect was electrifying—the face of the white man, worn with age and exposure to the elements—disturbing to him in some basic manner Arthur was unable to explain. He feared the stranger had been about to say something to him, ask him some question (a simple direction, perhaps?) his mouth opening, but then, like Arthur's leg, frozen in that vulnerable position—silent, yet foreboding. A chill ran up Arthur's spine as his eyes locked with those of the unknown individual; then his foot hit the ground, as the stranger—clearly deformed in body and soul—turned again toward his companion.

Arthur increased his pace, determined not to glance back at the figures in front of the tobacco seller's stall. There was something vaguely disconcerting about the incident, momentary though it had been. What was happening to him that he shunned all forms of human communication? For months now, there had been a change in his habits of living. He no longer involved himself with other human beings, but shirked his responsibilities, increasingly withdrawing into himself. In the months since Hester had informed him of her condition, he had retreated into himself, avoided contact with his parishioners and strangers alike, shunned even the role of the Good Samaritan. Probably all the figure at the stall had desired was a simple acknowledgment, a sentence or two welcoming him back to the world of the civilized, but Arthur had failed him. Nonetheless, in his walk back to the Widow Finney's, Arthur avoided any direct countenance with the people who passed him on the streets.

Though he would have preferred to retain his solitude, by the time he returned to his chambers the Widow Finney had set the table with their morning repast. Reluctantly, he sat down across from her and said the morning grace.

"They say that Mistress Prynne will be forced to remain on the scaffold until she reveals the name of her accomplice," the widow began, jolting Arthur back to the realities of the day. His body trembled, and he placed his hand over his breast, fearing that he might suffer from an attack of angina.

"That is not so," he managed to reply, after he had gathered his thoughts. "Who told you that?"

"One of the sellers in the market," the good woman replied.

"That is . . . that is incorrect," Arthur mumbled. "She will stand there for three hours, to be certain, as was agreed upon, but no longer than that."

"And will they ask her to reveal the name of her lover?"

"She will be asked that again," Arthur replied, forcing food into his mouth to conceal his nervousness. "A final time." A final time, which, if Hester could withstand, would release him from subsequent fears of public questioning. He swallowed a mouthful of tea, burning his tongue in the process.

"A goodly number of people are waiting to defile her when she ascends the platform this afternoon," the widow informed him.

Arthur brought his cup down upon the table with such force that some of the contents spilled over the edge. "What?" he asked with such fervor he feared the widow would notice the pain in his voice. In his concern for Hester's welfare, he had managed to stretch the one-syllable word into three or four.

"There are people who say she will be stoned when she ascends the platform."

"For whatever reason? Have they no mercy on this pitiful creature?"

"They fear that she has not been disciplined as severely as she should, that the punishment has not been molded to match the extent of her crime."

"Womenfolk, you say?" Arthur asked, trying to conceal the fury in his voice.

"Yes, only women—busybodies—who believe that she has brought humiliation to all of her sex."

He paused a moment, then asked his landlady, "And how do you feel about Hester Prynne's punishment, Mistress Finney?"

"It is sufficient for her transgressions, but I am an old woman, and no one pays any attention to me."

"Those hussies will be stopped," Arthur informed her, surprised by the strength that had returned to his voice.

To any outsider, the raucous noises from the crowd below him would have belied a day of public merrymaking, some Dionysiac or satyric rite rather than the more solemn occasion the community elders had intended. The market was swollen with Boston's citizenry, farmers and their families from the countryside, and here and there a group of domesticated Indians. Even a number of sailors from the English ship docked in the harbor had joined in the general mêlée. The din—though perhaps not one of drunkenness or licentiousness, given the austere temperament of Puritan belief—rose up above the crowd and prohibited Arthur Dimmesdale and his companions (seated on the balcony of the meetinghouse) from carrying on any sustained conversation. For that small blessing he was relieved.

In front of the meetinghouse, at one end of the market opposite First Church stood the public scaffold, which Hester would shortly ascend and stand upon with her child for the three hours' duration—the final stage of her public confrontation with her punishers. Though the Reverend Dimmesdale was not a novice to the field of law enforcement—indeed, nor were his companions seated next to him—as his eyes in his newly repaired glasses swept across the mass of people surrounding the scaffold and took in, at the angle above it, the steeples of First Church, for the first time he experienced some inchoate discomfiture. Rising up into the cloud-streaked sky, the spire created the impression of being buttressed by the monstrous legs of the public scaffold. Though it was only an optical illusion from his angle of vision, it was as if the church was mounted upon the scaffold, as if whatever ethereal and invisible ideal the holy edifice suggested by its towers grasping at the unknown, its roots were caught in the rigidity of the more restricted world composed of public whippings and humiliations. From the rain earlier in the week, Arthur noticed mud spattered on two of the massive legs of the scaffold—the filth and mire of the earth—threatening to climb up the secular structure and contaminate the body religious.

As the sun disappeared behind a cloud, the throng of citizens appeared to be shocked as if by some kind of magnetic force: their voices increased to near fervent intensity, and Arthur heard one of the women below him loudly proclaim, "Peace. Mistress Prynne approaches." The uproar from the square began to lessen; the movement of the bodies slowed like a child's top about to cease its gyrations and keel over. Slowly, to Arthur's surprise, there was dead silence; the only sound the rustle of leaves in the breeze, the chirrupping of birds, and the barking of a dog from one of the side streets that led to the public market.

Arthur glanced at the other dignitaries seated near him, conscious of the rigidity of their bodies, their necks strained to catch a glimpse of Hester Prynne. He could hear subdued breathing coming from the leaders around him though his own respiration had nearly ceased. Then he glanced back at the end of Prison Lane, guarded by curious citizens eagerly awaiting Hester Prynne's approach.

The cloud in the sky that had been protecting them from the rays of the early afternoon sun was abruptly whisked away as if by the hand of God, pulling it aside in order to assure visibility for the auspicious moment at hand. The denizens, who minutes before had blocked the entrance to Prison Lane, moved quickly back, as Hester Prynne appeared at the edge of Market Square, the scarlet letter on her breast—highlighted by a fine outline of gold thread—momentarily reflecting in the sun, threatening to blind Arthur Dimmesdale. He blinked his eyes, wondering if he were having a vision. But, no, it was Hester, with the child held in her arms, slightly to one side as if by intent so all could marvel at the emblem on her breast.

Proudly, she approached the scaffold below him, flanked by the town beadle, Master Brackett, and the officials assigned to her retinue. In spite of Hester's coarse garments, there was nothing in her demeanor to suggest that she was a prisoner in their midst. Rather, in all her majesty and stateliness, she appeared to head some regal procession of a courtly pageant in some far-off peaceful land. But, then, to Arthur's surprise, the crowd burst forth with raucous jeers and heckles, as if Boston's citizens had also recognized the majestic implications of the silence and were determined that Hester should be brought back to the world of her own undoing.

Hester ascended the platform with such caution and poise one would have thought the child in her arms were made of glass. The cries and jeers that moments before had suggested the unchecked rule of mob violence suddenly came to a dead stop, and when Arthur lifted his eyes away from Hester on the scaffold, he noticed that Governor Bellingham had raised his hand, imploring restraint from the crowd. The silence continued. Hester positioned herself near the center of the scaffold, at a stance slightly to the dignitaries' advantage, her head raised evenly with the balcony in front of her where Arthur and the other officials were emplanted. There was no expression on her face except a kind of natural radiance suggesting royalty and innocence. At the sign from the town beadle, the three hours of Hester's punishment had begun.

In the hours that followed, Arthur found his thoughts flowing back to the earlier stages of his relationship with Hester Prynne, collecting and sorting images at random as if they could be grouped like pebbles one picks up on the beach and later categorizes according to size and shape. There was Hester Prynne, immediately in front of him, regally adorned with the scarlet letter, her long auburn hair hidden away inside her cap, her natural beauty no doubt startling may of the onlookers who had been expecting something more grotesque. Yet in his mind's eye, there was also Hester with her shoulders bare, the same dark tresses strewn upon a velvet blanket of pine needles and moss, her eyes sparkling even in the midst of the subdued light penetrating into their hidden retreat.

Hester publicly scorned, answering the questions Governor Bellingham asked her in his supercilious voice. Hester free and vivacious, tempting Arthur in the forest.

"But what will happen to us when your husband arrives?"

"That cannot be. He is lost at sea."

"But if he does return? If he has not perished in the depths or been set upon by Indians?"

"Then we will flee away where he will never find us. His power over me has ceased. From the moment I set eyes upon him, I never loved him and would not have agreed to the arrangement were it not for my poor father."

"But marriages are made in heaven, Hester. You have taken a sacred vow."

"There are things more sacred than heaven and your church can sanctify, Arthur. I cannot be a widow without being a wife first, waiting, waiting, waiting for seven years until such time the laws decide that I am free."

"Do you fear no power greater than those designed by men to correct their errant ways, Hester? No greater force that unites us and tempts us even at this very moment?"

"You are the only force that guides me, Arthur. No other power can be as great as you."

"I fear for your soul, Hester. And mine, too. I have known not how to act these recent weeks, nor where the path we journey upon will guide us. My life has not prepared me for these sudden events."

"All my waking moments, all of my life, I have waited for this. Can we not establish a separate union here—pure and free, away from the earthly entanglements that bind us to the colony?"

"A man cannot renounce his calling as easily as that, Hester. There are those whose claims upon me are as real as yours. I feel the drawstrings pulling at me, tightening, threatening to choke me further. You ask too much. There is no place we can flee where we will not be discovered. The church has its own dictates upon my body, as well as upon my soul."

"I hate the world you have permitted to encroach upon you. It has made you a slave in a heathen land. Sometimes I curse the day my ship landed in this foreign clime."

"It is my calling and my life, Hester."

"It is no life for any mortal man."

"Reverend Dimmesdale?" the voice repeated, crashing in upon the world of Arthur's making. "Reverend Dimmesdale, are you ill?" one of the elders asked him, shaking his arm. "Do you need something to drink? Methinks the sun is too intense for you. It burns us like moths over a flame."

"I am all right," Arthur replied, the twitch in his body as much an attempt to shake off his memories as a symptom of his growing discontent. "I thank you for your kind concern, Master Simonds. This heat will do Hester Prynne's child no good. It is Hester and her child who should be offered a vessel of water."

He glanced back at the scaffold, at Hester and Pearl—madonna and child, fused together as though they had been sculpted of marble. The world around the scaffold had returned to some degree of normalcy. Though the size of the crowd had in no way decreased since Hester Prynne had begun her public exposure, many of the witnesses had returned to their own best interests, buying and selling as if this were a normal market day.

Another conversation dominated Arthur's mind:

"The Devil wears many disguises, Hester. At times I even fear he has sent you to lead me away from the path of goodness and salvation. How can I be certain that the Devil has not stolen away your soul?"

"There are worse fates to tempt us than the Devil, Arthur. Oh, I would readily have signed a pact with the Devil a hundred times over on that horrid crossing of the ocean, if he had only shown his face before me. But the Devil has larger catches at his disposal than you or me. For twelve weeks that ship floundered on the sea, bringing with it living hell—nay, an inferno far more discomforting than any god could ever have manufactured for our earthly punishment.''

''And you were tempted to sign a pact with the Black Man, catapulting you into the flames of eternity?''

''Yes, and would have done so and worse—jumped over the edge and into the waters—but for one determination.''

''What was that, Hester?''

''That I would be free forever from my husband, if I survived the endless voyage. No water, no food, five weeks overdue in a rat-infested dinghy that made skeletons of us all, and cannibals of more than one—all for the sake of God's sacred convenant in the New World.''

''But you survived and lived to tell the tale, Hester. Certainly that cannot be regarded as anything but a sign of the Lord's bounteous goodness. He tests us eternally, every moment of our lives—as even now.''

''But I did not give in to those temptations you speak about so obliquely, Arthur. And there were those, too, even on the ship.''

''You mean that there were men who desired you?''

''Ah, many—including the captain himself, the wretched beast, with promises of food and water from his private stocks, if I would but return the favor.''

''You never told me that before.''

''There was no reason, Arthur. Though I be several years your junior, and still a novice to the life in this wild country, there are experiences that I have already had that can never reach the depths of discomfort I experienced on that ship—or even my life before that. That was my testing and the preparation for our relationship now. Yours will be simpler by far.''

A voice screamed in the silence, shattering Arthur's reverie and returning him to the more immediate world. Though he clasped his hands over his ears reflexively to curtail the cry of pain and ducked as if he were attempting to parry a blow from some invisible sword, he knew that the shriek was only in his mind, a figment of his own troubled imagination. Governor Bellingham had talked to Hester Prynne, argued with her to reveal the name of her lover, and Arthur—who knew he would shortly be called upon to join in the debate—found himself the victim of uncontrollable thoughts and confessions that entered and exited his mind with cometic fury; naked bodies locked together, limbs sticking randomly into the air in suggestive positions, wild cries of ecstasy and passion.

"In the forest we are free, Arthur. No one can ever discover us here, though they walk right past us. If you doubt me, let me remain here unclothed when you bring old Reverend Wilson for a walk on yonder path. He will not see me in this dark, dense haven."

"Have you no shame, Hester? Would you bring everything out into the light of day? I fear your recklessness will lead to our undoing. Was I not the one who found you bathing naked in the brook? What if it had been someone else?"

"Ah, you did. But that was my intent, knowing the pathway of your forest sojourns. Had I been more secretive, you would never had discovered this hiding place in a thousand moons."

"You know I fear the forest, Hester, even now—perhaps more than before. We can never be totally safe here; we must always be on guard."

"The forest brings us freedom, Arthur—nothing more. For that there is always some price to pay, some string attached."

Then Hester screamed out uncontrollably, as though the Black Man had appeared over Arthur's shoulder.

"Brother, are you all right?" the Reverend Wilson asked him. "If you are able, it is best for you to question the woman and exhort from her a confession."

Arthur rose from his seat among the officials and stepped to the edge of the balcony. "I have come here to confess—Hester Prynne of her crimes."

"There can be no crime where there is no malice, Arthur, no victim or intent. We are guilty of nothing except expressing our love for one another."

"Punish her for her crimes! Punish her for her crimes!" The crowd around the scaffold had broken into a wild chant, repeating the request frantically as Hester stood there, the only source of illumination in Arthur's troubled world.

AD, AD, AD, Arthur Dimmesdale, Arthur Dimmesdale, Arthur Dimmesdale. Screams of pain and sorrow.

"Speak, woman! And give your child a father!"

It is I alone who have come to save you. I alone who survived to tell the tale. Here in my guilt and my salvation.

"Never!"

"Punish her for her crimes!"

"Arthur, we must flee from this wretched place to the safety of some inner isle where no one will ever be able to identify us or question our whereabouts."

"She has coupled with the Devil," Governor Bellingham whispered in Arthur's ear, "and that is why she refuses to give in to our demands. Perhaps if we question her privately, she will describe the lustful encounter for our edification and amusement." Governor Bellingham winked at Arthur and lowered his hand to his privates and made an obscene gesture.

"What you need is a wife to warm your bed at night, Arthur," Reverend Wilson muttered privately to his assistant pastor. "This is no country for a man to be proud of his bachelorhood," and the good minister pinched Arthur's right buttock.

"Take off your cassock, Arthur. No one will disturb us here. We are safe from all the thousand eyes of our countrymen."

"Only the eye of God, Hester, which can see through everything."

"All the more reason, then, to remove our garments, since we are naked as the day we entered this world. Nakedness is nothing to be ashamed of."

"I hate the whiteness of my flesh—have fled it all my life. This garment makes me whole and complete, reminds me daily that I am better than the beasts of the earth."

"But flesh as white as yours, Arthur, is also purity."

"Burn her as a witch. She rides through the sky at night with Mistress Hibbins, the witch-lady."

"The child too, the Devil's mistress and her daughter. Punish them or the entire village will be polluted. How can we raise our children in her presence?"

"Let he who is so impure cast the first stone," Arthur exhorted the crowd, aware that he had said the opposite of what he intended. But there was no response to his condemnation, for wherever he looked couples had paired off and were engaging in the most blatant debauchery. The Devil had surely fled from Merrymount and turned the market into a center of licentiousness.

"Confess your lover, Hester, and give your child a name."

"Never. That is our secret."

AD, AD, AD.

"Come join with goodly Reverend Wilson and me at the back of the balcony, Reverend Dimmesdale," Governor Bellingham invited him, pulling on Arthur's cassock, "and we will show you that there is more than one way to skin a cat."

Arthur blushed at the suggestion, but found it impossible to remove his eyes from the Governor and Reverend Wilson, their bodies locked together in mad embrace.

"Hester, you know that I am inexperienced in such matters and fear my naïveté will only lead to greater embarrassments for both of us."

"Nature need never be embarrassed, Arthur. The mask we wear in public is by far the most self-conscious one. Follow where I lead you, Arthur, Arthur, Arthur."

"Never!"

Whether it was Governor Bellingham's gesture or the cries from the child at Hester's side, Arthur could not be certain. But suddenly there was order again where moments before there had been chaos and confusion, and only the wails coming from the child's open mouth. Perhaps the body collective had decided that the afternoon's amusements were over, for here and there Arthur could detect that people were leaving the market, scattering from their former positions at the foot of the scaffold.

Then, to his surprise, Arthur spotted the mysterious figure from his morning walk: the white man and his Indian companion, standing somewhat removed from the rest of the people in the market. When the child broke the silence with yet another scream, and Arthur glanced back at Hester on the scaffold, he was surprised to notice the troubled expression on her face, for she too was looking at the mysterious stranger and was unable to conceal the extent of her alarm. Surely there is something amiss here, Arthur thought to himself, wondering if anyone else had detected some mark of change in Hester Prynne's countenance. When he turned to his companions, however, Arthur discovered that they were engaged in polite conversation with one another, oblivious of the exchange of glances that had taken place in front of them.

When he looked for the stranger a moment later, it was too late. The figures had disappeared as if they had fallen through some hole in the ground. Then Pearl's cries broke the silence still again, and the town beadle announced that the duration of Hester's public ignominy had come to an end.

Arthur hastened forward, head held determinedly at an angle that would once again discourage conversation with any of his parishioners. It was late in the afternoon; the procession had ended and Hester and her child had been escorted to the prison for one last consultation before their release. The crowd was dispersed, except for a few stragglers—older people, families with children who had used Hester's disgrace as a moral lesson. Feigning illness, Arthur had broken away from the governor's entourage, about to celebrate the end of the day at the gentleman's mansion.

Arthur hurried up High Street, past the entrance to the spring that fed Winthrop's Marsh, past the turn into Milk Street, the leaden weight of his legs, even his clerical garments, holding him to the ground. Hester's voice—clear and determined—droned in his ears:

"In the forest we are free, Arthur. No one will ever discover us here, though they walk right past us. The forest is all we have."

His heart ached with growing humiliation, a sense of defeat. Thrice he had failed Hester, denied her existence as the complement to his body. They should have fled the country when she first became aware of her altered state. The day of the child's birth, he should have broken the silence and made his identity known. And, now, he had missed his third and final chance to ease his melancholy conscience. Hester was free, and he had become a prisoner in the midst of his own beloved parishioners, his relationship with them, henceforth, nothing but a fraud. Each day would take him closer to the final reckoning point, remove him further from the people who loved him and to whom he professed to administer. Each moment his isolation would increase until his pent-up agonies exploded and the Devil carried him away for an interminable residence in Hell.

And what of Hester—why had he failed her at every station to the cross? Hester, who had stood there stoically enduring the obscenities of the crowd. Hester, who had certainly expected more of him, some simple gesture, even the faintest clue that he cared for someone besides himself. How had she endured these months of public wrath and scorn without cursing his very existence, his spinelessness, his selfishness? How had he failed to discover some way of communicating his sympathies with her?

What were they to do now? Could they ever meet again without someone suspecting their true relationship? Were they both to endure a future existence separate from each other? Had their love been reduced to a vacuity like this? Arthur did not know how he could endure such a relationship in future years, seeing Hester and the child walking down a street and being unable to stop and communicate with them—worse, unable to hold the child, *his* child, by the hand and guide it down the maze that certainly represented its future. How could they pass on the street like that, no more than strangers in a troubled land?

Arthur ran through the woods, searching for the place of his secret encounters with Hester, but it was to no avail. He was lost; he could not locate it. Autumn, winter, spring, and now summer had returned, each season bringing with it change and permutation. Their grotto had disappeared. Some woodsman had forged a path through the trees and chopped down the haven of their escape. Or was the Devil playing a trick on him, hiding the retreat which certainly ought to stand before him? Arthur charged through the forest, pushing aside branches, trampling flowers and shoots, frenzied like a wild boar, but nowhere could he locate their den of iniquity. Hester was right: no one would ever be able to discover their hiding place; it had vanished from the face of the earth.

Stopping abruptly, rage and anger exuding from every pore of his flesh, Arthur realized what had happened, the full context for the events of the last year and more: there never had been a safe retreat from the outside world where Hester and he were safe from discovery. There never had been a sacred meeting place in the forest where they had sworn their love for each other. The universe they thought they had created was an illusion; it had never existed. Hester was wrong; their lives were not a private matter. Man—a communal animal, just one step above the beasts—did not have a separate room to hide away his egocentric behavior. He was bound to the mass—to the whole. Arthur stood panting, one arm holding on to a tree for support, the other dangling lifeless at his side. He would have to return to the whole, the collective body from which he had erroneously thought that he was separate.

Yet staring ahead, in front of him and slightly off to one side, Arthur discovered the entrance to their past retreat: the shapes, the colors of the trees, more common than he had remembered them—the perfect disguise, of course, for any passerby unaware of the dominion hidden away inside. Arthur marched ahead, pushed a shrub aside, and entered the dark cavern of their past existence, amazed at its sameness nearly a year later.

Although he did not know exactly what he expected to discover within the grotto or what painful memories it would conjure up from the past, when he sat down on the carpet of leaves and pine needles, he thought of one possible act that might restore communication with Hester. If he could leave some mark, some sign, within their private cocoon, Hester would know he had not totally failed her—had not given her up completely. Hester, he knew, would return here also—perhaps was even thinking about it at this very moment—knowing full well that it was the only arena in which they could meet again. As it was before, so it would be again—perhaps not exactly the same, but they could at least establish some measure of communication, if that only meant leaving messages hidden for each other.

But Arthur had nothing on his person to write upon or with, no identification to leave as a mark of his concern. What could he do? How was Hester to learn that he had not forsaken her? It was important that his sign be made immediately, since Hester, released from all these months of confinement, was free to walk where she chose. Surely she would come here within a matter of days, perhaps even hours, and they could begin to plot their escape from Boston and its confines. It was not too late. But what could he do: form two sticks into a cross? The letter *A?* The idea was perverse, and he trembled at the thought of it.

Then it came to him as, momentarily, he lifted his hand to his neck and touched the collar that encircled his throat. In an instant, he had unbuttoned the collar from his garment, removed it from his neck, and tied it securely to a branch within their retreat. When Hester discovered it, she would know immediately what it meant and what to expect. They could meet and discuss their solution for the future. They could fly away and be together forever. The interminable darkness that had fallen over their lives these many months was about to lift.

He returned to the village, his spirits noticeably calmed. He walked through the streets, no longer avoiding communication with his fellow citizens, no longer afraid to look them directly in the face. The clouds in the sky had lifted, just as a veil over his own troubled soul had been removed by some higher force, still watching over him after all these terrible months. For the first time in days, he thought it might still be possible to find happiness with Hester and little Pearl. God was back in control of Arthur's universe.

Then the world shattered once again, for even before he had returned to his rooms, Arthur met the town beadle who informed him that Master Brackett had been searching for him. ''The child of Hester Prynne has been taken seriously ill, and is not expected to live,'' the town messenger informed him. ''Master Brackett seeks your advice in these matters, but he has been unable to locate you.''

''I will go to the prison immediately,'' Arthur told him, hastening down Prison Lane and spying a group of villagers standing outside the ominous building.

As he reached the crowd in front of the prison, he was just in time to see Master Brackett disappear inside the structure. Walking unevenly beside him was a darker figure, dressed in a strange mixture of clothing from the heathen and the civilized worlds. A shiver went up Arthur's spine as he recognized the shadow that followed Master Brackett as the hump-shouldered stranger in the market, no longer flanked by his Indian companion.

''Who is that with Master Brackett?'' Arthur asked one of the bystanders in front of the public building.

''Some stranger who claims to be a doctor of physic, though if you ask me, he looks like the Devil.''

Chapter Five

Until the day of Hester's public scorn, Arthur had given little thought to his future, to his role as spiritual leader of his little flock of Puritan sinners. Preoccupied with quotidian matters, he had avoided a glance into the future—inwardly, perhaps, refusing to concede the possibility of continued distress. In short, he had been unfaithful not only to Hester and her child, but also to himself, accepting the mawkish view that all would be aright, that life would revert to its ordered path, the way it had been before his involvement with Hester. Pity those men whose eyes always turn in upon themselves.

At first, when there was no mark or message from Hester left in their secret meeting place (or even any evidence that she had visited the retreat), Arthur took it calmly enough, assuming that Hester had decided to exercise even more caution than he. Patience was what was required, and patience was what he would demonstrate. It would only be a matter of time, and then Hester would reestablish communication with him. But weeks, and then months, passed with no indication that Hester had returned to their lair, and the collar he had left there grew moldy from the summer rains and humidity and then shriveled from the autumn drought. By early November, the bleached piece of cloth hung limply from the branch, looking more like a discarded ribbon from some maiden's bonnet than a clerical collar. And still there was no sign from Hester.

It was not a matter of Arthur's being unfamiliar with Hester's altered life. Their patterns of living overlapped (as was perhaps inevitable in such a small community) and Arthur assumed that

Hester was as aware of his existence as he was of hers. It was, rather, a question of his belated recognition of what had happened. Slowly he came to realize that he could not go on living as he had before, his life horribly sealed off from others around him. His ministry was certainly a ticket into the troubled lives of his parishioners, but it was also a journey into the self, removing him always at a safe distance from anything but the spiritual involvement of the members of his flock. Though he had yet to recognize it, he was a man who had fallen out of contact with the temporal world. The spiritual support he administered to his followers (like little dollops of soup to the hungry) was predicated upon his moral hypochondria.

And what of Hester and her child during the early weeks and months after her release from confinement? Arthur had heard: shunned woman that she was, she accepted the burden that was her lot and merged back into the daily existence of her environment. With Pearl, she settled into an abandoned cottage at the outskirts of the village, announcing to sinner and saint alike her services as a seamstress, the letter A on her bosom (the only adornment she permitted on her otherwise drab garments), the ironic advertisement of her skill and labor with her needle. Though she held faithfully to her demeanor as the penitent, it was not long before her talents overshadowed the symbol on her bosom and demands for her handiwork assured her a livelihood, the cottage she lived in with little Pearl becoming a satellite on Boston's hub, each dependent and in time relying upon the other.

For Arthur, the world was no longer so simply ordered. As the seasons chased one another with a fury familiar only to those who have lived in New England, increasingly Arthur became obsessed with his own private sin. It gnawed at his conscience, and daily became more visible as his physical condition. With winter, the colds, the sore throat, and the hacking cough returned, eating deeply into his respiratory system, at times with such persistence that it was impossible for him to complete his Sunday discourse—all to the disappointment of his listeners who considered his sermons to have achieved the pinnacle of brilliance. His body, racked by constant fever, grew lean like a willow, his skin discolored as if by jaundice. By spring, his parishioners were so concerned with his debilitated state they recommended to old Reverend Wilson that the assistant pastor of First Church be temporarily released from his duties—a suggestion Arthur declined, assuring his spiritual father that it was only a matter of time before warm weather would return and restore his body to its former vigor.

"I have always been given to little illnesses," he informed his elder, "ever since a child. I accept them for what they are: part of the nature of our living. These momentary disabilities will quickly pass."

Reverend Wilson recommended a purgative.

"I accept your advice," Arthur replied, but ignored the suggestion once he had left the confines of the older man's study, knowing full well the source of his own current disability: the invisible letter dominating his own psyche.

A word or two about Reverend Dimmesdale's earlier life may be germane here. As Arthur indeed told Reverend Wilson, he had always been a sickly child, reticent and melancholy. His father, a ship's captain, had disappeared at sea when Arthur was four years old, leaving the boy's mother an ample though dwindling inheritance for the upbringing of her children: Arthur and his two older sisters, Elizabeth (thirteen) and Maria Louise (eight). The boy grew up in a household dominated by females and imaginary illnesses, for after the news of the death of her husband, Mrs. Dimmesdale shut herself away in her room, for twenty years taking her meals alone, speaking little and suggesting even less. Arthur was left to the upbringing of his sisters, their own morbid thoughts projected from their mother's seclusion and sadness.

When he was nine, he injured his foot one day playing ball with some boys in the neighborhood he had lately befriended in an unsuccessful attempt to escape the confines of the ever-encroaching female world. The boyhood camaraderie was suddenly terminated, since Arthur became confined at home because of the crutches upon which he was forced to depend. For five years he remained a prisoner in the house, reading, playing with the family cat called Beelzebub, increasingly accepting the introspective, adult world. When freed at last of the crutches, his desire for contact with the outside world had been supplanted by the printed word and a growing pathological morbidity.

When summer returned to Arthur's body, he was temporarily able to convince his followers that his illnesses had departed. His cough had subsided; the sore throat and cold for the moment, at least, had burrowed underground. For a time, Arthur was able to deceive his parishioners into believing that all was well again; he could carry out the duties assigned to him. Indeed, several of his more devoted followers noted the extreme diligence with which Arthur pursued his tasks, especially (they observed) the vigor the young minister manifested in attempting to convert the Indian population. Reverend Dimmesdale was given to visiting these heathen peoples in their natural haunts in the forest, where increasingly he sojourned of an afternoon for several hours at a time. The exercise did him good, it was thought, whether or not it led to the conversion of a few unenlightened peoples.

As the reader may surmise, these walks in the forest had little to do with the salvation of the Native population, but were designed as Arthur's own curative treatment. They freed him of the dictates of his profession, made it possible for him to remove the mask he always wore among his parishioners. Yet when that mask was removed, the image of his former self was in no way restored, since there were in effect two sides to his predicament. The mask he wore in Boston, among the people of his flock, permitted him to present a face smoothed free of the deeper wrinkles that textured the hidden realities of his flesh. It was a means of survival, permitting Arthur to disguise the derangement which, if exposed, would lead to certain destruction. The deeply furrowed face he wore in the forest, though free of the necessity for deception, mirrored the furies of his soul, the inner tensions that were hidden away so carefully from others that only a trained physician would be able to speculate on their accumulative effect. In short, it was as if Arthur had donned some kind of Janus mask—the upturned mouth, worn in the village; the frown, in the forest. Both expressions were unnatural to his face.

There was, of course, another reason for Arthur's forest sojourns: his desire to meet with Hester Prynne. What better place that one outcast should meet another? Or so Arthur reasoned, failing to recognize that Hester's status was becoming more closely woven within the community's. Thus, although Arthur searched for Hester and Pearl in the forest, it was to no avail. More than a year after her public humiliation on the scaffold, there was still no evidence that she had ever returned to their hidden lair near the brook, though Arthur returned there periodically to search for signs of her. Though he spent afternoon following afternoon in the forest gloom, he did not encounter Hester and the child.

During the second year after Hester's ordeal on the scaffold, Arthur would see mother and child from time to time in the village itself—perhaps in the market when Hester came to do her bartering. Always, there was an invisible circle surrounding her—a radius of some ten feet or more—that separated mother and child from the town's other citizens. In that year Arthur also discovered a more objectified fear that confused his yearnings to meet and talk with Hester Prynne: Pearl, their child, walking alone, running along in front or behind her mother like a free spirit, frightened him.

To be sure, Arthur had always been aloof from children, never knowing exactly how to act in their presence; and children, identifying this hesitancy on his part, were in turn fearful of him. He wondered why children troubled him so. Were children simply small adults to be treated like their parents—as sinners all—or were they closer to God and, therefore, purer and uncorrupted? Did one talk to them as one talked to an adult? Or treat them as pets—as small objects more animal than human? Arthur did not know. He had never even had a clue, though he had tried both methods: holding and cuddling them (they usually cried) and talking to them about their salvation. Looking at Pearl tag along behind her mother, at times almost believing that she flew behind her, Arthur feared the growth of this child as much as he desired a confrontation with her mother. There was no way, he knew, that he could meet the mother without the daughter. She was, indeed, the irritant of their lives.

One day during the third summer after Pearl's birth, when Arthur had almost given up all expectation of meeting with Hester in the forest, his goal fell fleetingly within his grasp, but then vanished almost as quickly as it had materialized. It was a day like many of the others when he had walked randomly through the woods for several hours. Tired and melancholy as usual—the Janus mask firmly positioned in the downturned expression—he withdrew from the path on which he had been treading in order to rest his weary feet. Perhaps he had fallen asleep—or, more likely, he momentarily experienced an hallucination, wishfully desired; for before he knew it, Hester, followed by little Pearl, was walking down the pathway, coming in his direction.

Then, for some unknown reason—just as his dream was about to be fulfilled—instead of alerting them to his presence, he hid himself more secretly within the branches of a hemlock tree, over-grown with some parasitic vine. Perhaps it was the fear that Hester and Pearl were not alone but walking with some third party in the woods. He was not quite certain until the chance was gone. Hester passed him by, unaware of his presence, moving almost silently along the path. Then came Pearl, scampering along like some kind of exotic creature of the jungle (a unicorn perhaps?), unafraid of any other animal, loudly proclaiming her presence—her damage to the natural world curtailed only by her size.

When the child reached the area where Arthur had hidden himself, there was something quite irrational that told him to reach out and touch her, grab hold of her, and pull her into the woods and flee away with her. He refrained, of course, his whole body vibrating like some animal suffering from St. Vitus's dance, but as she passed him by, he pushed the branches aside and permitted his child to see him trembling there, framed within a cloak of leaves and pine needles. The child glanced in his direction, opened her mouth as if she were about to cry out to her mother, but instead stuck her tongue out at him, as he in turn merged back into the foliage. Then Arthur watched Pearl scamper along the pathway, toward her mother. He was surprised that she uttered no sound or cry of fear or recognition, nor was there any indication that a word would be said to her mother about the apparition she had observed.

At first, Arthur didn't know whether to be puzzled or pleased. He had failed in his attempt to communicate with Hester, yet he had derived a certain pride at the more symbolic level of contact he had made with Pearl. The child he had been so frightened of had demonstrated no fear of him at all. The forest appeared to harbor no demons for her, the greenwood which continually troubled him as an extension of the great unknown. Arthur knew quite well that if the same thing had happened to him as a child, he would have been panic-stricken for hours, yet this simple child was free of the illusions he, as an adult, had yet to conquer. What was the explanation for her tranquillity except that she was the antithesis of his own fear and sadness, the ubiquitous proof of his own dreadful sin?

Later, when he considered the incident in more detail, he was flooded with feelings of guilt and remorse. It was his own child he had played a trick upon in the forest, his own child who had failed to identify him. Did she mean so little to him? Would his relation-ship with his own daughter always be nothing more than a game of hide-and-seek? The child is father of the man, but in this case was the man the father of the child?

Several months later, when Arthur—along with Reverend Wilson and a number of other guests—was visiting Governor Bellingham, he had his first formal encounter with Hester and the child since the day of their release from prison. Present also at the meeting was old Roger Chillingworth—the mysterious personage Arthur had first observed on the day of Hester's public exposure—who had since made his residence in Boston, offering his services as a doctor of physic. The villagers had welcomed Chillingworth once his profession was known—a physician after all, no common catch for any of the New England villages. To tell the truth, the old doctor's esteem had spread quickly during the ensuing years, perhaps almost as rapidly as Arthur Dimmesdale's fame as a minister—medicine and religion not being exactly estranged from each other.

There were members of Arthur's little flock of Puritans (granted, women mostly) who had even suggested that their pastor should seek the advice of Roger Chillingworth to cure him of his repeated illnesses; and though these two gentlemen had spoken together a number of times during the past three years, Arthur thus far had avoided any direct discourse about his ailment with the old physician. "My illnesses are predictable and controllable," he had told Reverend Wilson a number of times, once again foiling those who most desired to aid in his physical improvement.

On the day that concerns us, when Arthur was listening to Governor Bellingham hold forth on the machinations of some recent tax law and when Arthur's mind in truth was wandering to other subjects, he suddenly heard a startling, high-pitched scream, not unlike those mysterious voices he had identified in the past, though their presence in the governor's mansion was more than perplexing. Unconsciously, Arthur moved his hands to his ears, as if that action would prevent any further sudden movement from disturbing the air. He was about to scream out in pain when the room was suddenly attacked by some flighty monster in bright plumage, shrieking at the top of its wits. The effect on everyone in the chamber was that of a miniature tornado suddenly swooping down upon them and turning everything topsy-turvy. But then the activity stopped as quickly as it had begun, and there stood the source of the discord in their midst: little Pearl. A moment later, Hester entered the governor's sitting room and announced her intention of discussing some private matter with the king's representative.

"It is the woman of the scarlet letter," Governor Bellingham proclaimed to his guests, as if the mark on Hester's breast needed some explication. And he added, "The explanation for the witchcraft in this little baggage." He pointed in Pearl's direction, just as the child moved toward the safety of her mother.

"It is my child of whom you speak so disapprovingly," Hester replied, the scarlet letter visibly moving from the palpitations of her heart.

"I fear this wild creature needs taming before it is too late and the Devil takes her in hand," the governor lectured, to Hester Prynne's noticeable chagrin.

"Though she is the personification of my duty," Hester replied, "she daily teaches me such lessons that can never be forgotten."

"Does the child know her catechism?" asked the governor, looking along old Reverend Wilson's trajectory.

Arthur glanced quickly in Hester's direction, and then at the others in the room, relieved to notice that all eyes were focused upon the scarlet woman. Then before Hester could reply to the governor's question, the sturdy gentleman continued, "Methinks the child should be raised by other hands—those that will give her a proper upbringing—for what can she learn from this fallen woman?"

"There is much that I can teach her," Hester replied, her voice still considerably shaken, as she pointed at the letter on her breast. "Even now, though she be a child, I can teach her the lessons of my experience whereby she will be far wiser and better equipped to meet the temptations of this earth."

Arthur trembled and moved his hand to his breast, knowing that once again he had failed to come to Hester's aid. For all the difference he made, he need not even have been present in the room with her. He had ceased to exist as a concerned human being. As Governor Bellingham and Reverend Wilson questioned the child, Arthur swooned, and he felt as if he were falling into some bottomless pit. Then he heard Hester's voice, imploring him to come to her support: "I beg you. Thou knewest me as my spiritual confessor—speak out for me. I must not lose my child . . ."

When he considered the matter later, Arthur was surprised at the suddenness of his defense of Hester Prynne. For the first time in more than three years he had acted in a manner befitting his former nature. He had not vacillated, not stood there unable to decide which foot to move forward, but had spoken emphatically in Hester's (and the child's) defense. He knew, of course, that there was an extenuating matter—the continued fear of his own exposure—heightened more than at any time in the last few years by the presence of the other dignitaries and the strange, haunting movements of little Pearl; for the child was the true catalyst for his supportive remarks, the flighty creature who seemed more at home in the air than on the ground.

"It was fear, Hester, that pulled me from my lethargy and drove me to act in your defense. I feared that you would turn against me and reveal to all of those present the true nature of our relationship. I feared that Pearl would fly up around my neck and never let loose."

"Your fears would not be realized in ten thousand years, Arthur," Hester replied.

"I know that now, Hester, but your actions have always been motivated by love, whilst mine have been those of a man afraid. The difference between us, as I finally understand it, is that you act first and by your emotions are guided. My flaw is one of reaction, always based on the fear of discovery. It is the slower and usually more painful modus vivendi."

It was one of his imaginary conversations with Hester Prynne, beginning later in the day after he had left the governor's mansion and Hester had been permitted to retain the custody of her child. If he could not meet with her privately, then he would talk to her anyway, carry on little corrective discussions in his mind, analyzing his weaknesses and his shortcomings.

"You oversimplify the matter, Arthur. You are too hard on yourself. Our roles are not the same. Whether from fear or love, the fact is that you acted—and Pearl is still mine."

"It would not have happened if I had not looked up at the coat of armor displayed in the governor's sitting room and seen my own reflection emblazoned thereon, my own troubled expression looking back at me with your scarlet letter on my breast. I was frightened, Hester, lest Reverend Wilson or even old Roger Chillingworth should glance in that direction and see what I was staring at."

"It was an illusion, Arthur, or perhaps some kind of phantasm— our visages juxtaposed on the coat of mail—no doubt caused by the excitement of the moment."

"Perhaps, but I acted only out of the fear that others would see what I was seeing and had to draw their attention away from the demonic object. So I talked, rapidly, in your stead, and if you ask me now what I stated in your defense, I could not repeat it though my life depended upon it.''

"My life did depend on it, Arthur, and that is all that matters. Pearl is still mine. Still ours.''

Chapter Six

Roger Chillingworth was prowling around Arthur Dimmesdale's room: an ominous blurred shape silently stalking the fantastical. It was totally dark, sometime in the middle of the night, though from a candle that was burning outside in the hall, Arthur could just barely determine the older man's cautious movements. Arthur had opened his eyes a fraction of an inch and squinted, hoping the physician would not discover that he was being watched. Although it was difficult to control his breathing and the rapid beating of his heart, Arthur could hear the older man's erratic breaths. They sounded a little like a lopsided wheel on a horse cart, smooth and quiet until it hit the defective portion and then produced a momentary increase in sound.

Arthur watched Chillingworth poke around his clothing in his cupboard as if he were looking for some hidden document or valuable possession. Moisture broke out on Arthur's brow, the coursing of his blood increasing so rapidly that he could hear it rushing through his ears. Every few moments, Roger Chillingworth would turn in Arthur's direction, hold in his breath and listen attentively for the slightest mark of consciousness from the body in the bed. Then, apparently satisfied that Arthur was asleep, the older man would continue his searching, as if he were some kind of ordinary household thief rummaging for the family jewels.

Arthur watched the ghostly shape, wondering how long the episode would continue. How long could he feign his slumber? What was this man looking for in his room in the middle of the night? How would the scene end? Then, shortly, Roger Chillingworth left the wardrobe and crossed the room to the desk, where Arthur was no longer able to observe him. Arthur lay in bed, attempting to imagine what would happen next, and then deep within his chest he felt a cough forming in the soft tissues of his lungs, the mucus agitating him with such persistence that it was a little as if his neck and chest were held in the grip of some great beast, slowly tightening around him. He knew the cough was going to erupt, that there was nothing he could do to prevent the spasm taking over and jolting his body with unchecked fury. Then Roger Chillingworth would realize that he was being watched.

Arthur coughed, his body and his head shifting from the explosion to a position from which it might be possible to continue observing Roger Chillingworth, so he closed his eyes in case the prowler was looking at him. Though he could not see him, Arthur knew that the intruder was quietly waiting to determine if the man in the bed had been awakened. The game continued. Roger Chillingworth stood rigidly in his tracks waiting for Arthur to fall back into a deep slumber; Arthur lay motionless, afraid to open his eyes even the slightest bit. Time passed—probably only a few minutes, though Arthur felt he had lain there for hours—certainly it would soon be morning. Roger Chillingworth was so silent that Arthur could not even hear his breathing, and moments later he began to wonder if all of this weren't a dream, something he had been imagining.

But it was not one of Arthur's nightmares, or one of his frequent visions; Roger Chillingworth was snooping around his room in the middle of the night. The process began again: Arthur opened his eyes imperceptibly, he hoped, and tried to focus on the obscure shape in the hint of light coming from outside the room. The throb continued in his ears and his temples; he could again hear the older man's irregular respiration. Arthur felt the accumulation of perspiration on his forehead, fearing that the older man would realize he was not asleep. Should he cough again and make it appear that he was about to wake up? Should he intentionally move his body or make some sound that would cause Roger Chillingworth to flee? Arthur didn't know what to do. He wondered how much longer the intrigue would continue. He was uncomfortable, afraid to turn to a new position; he imagined that sores were forming on his back, like some patient confined for weeks and months to a sickbed.

Then he heard movements again and knew by the shadow before him that the older man had approached the bed and was standing above him, observing him prone on his mattress. Arthur considered closing his eyes completely, but his curiosity was so strong that he left them open a tiny slit. The blur above him was like some dark vulture he feared might smother him in his sleep. Certainly the perspiration on his forehead would betray his alertness.

Roger Chillingworth reached down and lifted up the sheet that covered Arthur in his bed, then slowly drew it back until it was below Arthur's waist where he let it gently fall. Then—horrified—Arthur could feel the older man pull at his nightshirt and begin to raise it up, lifting it away from his body. Arthur opened his eyes, cleared his throat, one hand moving toward his face to rub his eyes. The older man was the first to speak.

"Reverend Dimmesdale, are you in pain? I heard your cries in the night and thought you might be in need of medical assistance." Roger Chillingworth moved back a little to a safer distance. "Methinks you must have a fever—your brow is bathed in perspiration," and before Arthur could say anything, the older man momentarily touched his forehead, reached out for his right hand, and began to take his pulse.

"I . . . I do not know," Arthur replied, sitting up on one elbow. "I must have been dreaming."

"We have no control over our dreams," Roger Chillingworth told his patient gravely, though he appeared to be concentrating on counting the beats of the younger man's pulse.

"I think I am all right," Arthur replied hesitantly, anxious to draw his wrist away from the older man. He was repelled by the touch of the physician's flesh upon his own. "It was nothing—just some temporary unpleasantness. Fever I think," and he reached for his glasses at the stand by the side of his bed.

He placed them on his nose and looked more directly at the intruder, still holding his wrist. It seemed to him that Roger Chillingworth's finger was so hot that it might singe his skin. How could the old man talk of fever when his own flesh gave off a burning sensation like that? What would his pulse reveal, since it was certainly beating faster than normal from the excitement of the past few moments. Arthur glanced down at his nightshirt, relieved to see that it still covered his flesh, and with his left hand he lifted the sheet so that it protected him once again.

"The perspiration always tells us that the fever has broken," Roger Chillingworth replied, dropping Arthur's hand as if it were some foreign object that might contaminate him. "There is nothing wrong; it is normal. Do you remember what you were dreaming?"

"I do not remember anything," Arthur lied, "except crying out in my sleep, and then the next thing I knew you were here at the side of my bed."

"A pity. Our dreams sometimes tell us things we should know about ourselves. I learned these observations during the months I lived with the Indians. They place great stock in their dreams. You must try to remember yours—write them down, if necessary. Tell them to me and I will help you discover the source of your illness."

"I am not ill," Arthur replied, perhaps a little more emphatically than he should. He could not help noticing that the older man was not dressed in a nightshirt, but was wearing everyday clothing. "There is nothing I can tell you that you do not already know."

"I can be of no help, if you have forgotten some little incident or story that may be important, something you may have failed to recollect. What can I report to your parishioners as long as you persist in keeping secrets from me? I can be of no help to you that way."

Arthur trembled at the thought of the recent changes in his life: the Widow Finney's death, his subsequent move into more spacious quarters with the Widow Kellings, followed by Roger Chillingworth's own shift in lodgings—at the insistence of his congregation—into the chamber next to his own.

"I remember nothing else, nothing that I have not already told you."

"All in good time—we will see. Just let me give you something to help you sleep. You are still shivering, and I fear you will not be able to sleep without the aid of a sedative." Roger Chillingworth loped out of Arthur's room, the light from the candle in the hallway casting an elongated shadow through the minister's doorway.

What an ugly man he is, Arthur thought to himself, dreading the older man's return.

When he awakened in the morning—much later than he had intended because of the sedative the leech had insisted that he take—Arthur pondered over the events of the night. Was there no longer any escape for him, even in the privacy of his own room? Had he become the object of observation not only every minute of his waking day but also during the night? He would have to find some way of concealing his restless nights from Roger Chillingworth and the Widow Kellings, some way of fastening his door so that no one could enter his room. That would be no simple matter since there was no lock on the door to separate him from the rest of the house, and he knew of no way he could have one placed there without calling attention to himself and making matters worse. But Roger Chillingworth must not enter his room during the night again, since Arthur knew there was no way he could control his nocturnal paroxysms. What if he had cried out in the night? What if he had called for Hester? How would he even know?

He breakfasted with no enthusiasm, but at the Widow Kellings's insistence—he would have preferred to leave the household for the sanctity of his study at First Church, or take a walk in the forest. Roger Chillingworth appeared to be nowhere about, for which Arthur could only feel relieved, since he did not know what he would be able to say to the older man who had already learned more of his private affairs than Arthur had ever intended. What could he do to avoid another night of fear and trembling?

After breakfast—at the widow's reminder—Arthur prepared for the ritual of his bath, a weekly event he had come to loathe. His body was still fatigued, his skin loose and oily from the restless night. After the water had been boiled and poured into the wooden tub and he entered the bathing closet, he removed his nightshirt and lowered himself into the warm water, still clothed in his undergarment. To his surprise, the steam from the water and the intensity of the heat itself refreshed him, clearing the miasma in his brain. He scrubbed himself vigorously as if he could bathe away all the burdens of his troubled life, as if he could wash away the incrustations of his flesh. When he washed the areas between his legs, he closed his eyes so he would not see the flesh through the opaque cloth and tried to think of other matters, purer thoughts; and when he finished bathing—afraid to sit in the warm water and enjoy the pleasures of immersion—he avoided the tiny mirror the widow had nailed up on the wall of the garderobe. After he had pulled his nightshirt back over his body, he removed the saturated nether garment and wrung it out. He must not be tempted by images of the flesh, even those of his own body.

He returned to his room, closing the door behind him, relieved that Roger Chillingworth did not appear to be about.

Though it was already later than the time he usually departed for First Church, he was in no hurry to leave his room now that he had established his privacy. He could remember no official duties with the parish until later in the afternoon, so he decided to lie down on his bed for a few moments since his sleep during the night had been so interrupted.

When he awoke somewhat later, he was aware of a burning sensation on his chest and he knew that he had been scratching his flesh in his sleep. It itched as if it had been bitten by an insect—a mosquito, or a spider, perhaps, which had stung him in more than one place. He rubbed his chest through his sleeping shirt, but the itch was only exacerbated. He climbed out of bed and—after checking to see that no one was in the hallway—returned to the bathing closet where he could examine his chest in the only mirror he was aware of in the house. With the door closed behind him, Arthur pulled his nightshirt over his head, and quickly positioned himself in front of the mirror so that only the upper portion of his torso would be visible.

He was immediately horrified at his discovery, for there on his chest—slightly to one side—was the scarlet letter, faintly etched, to be sure, but obvious beyond any question. Arthur knew that he was not imagining some temporary inflammation caused by the recent scratching; it was clearly a large letter A, transmogrified to his flesh. It would be immediately apparent to anyone who examined his bare chest. What particularly disturbed him was that the image in the mirror reversed nothing—as it would have if it had been some letter such as a B or a C. The A was still an A in the mirror image, and would always remain unalterable by any method of refraction.

What could he do? He stood there transfixed, staring at the emblem on his breast. It was as if the world had stopped moving and there were no sounds to inform him that life outside the closet in which he stood in this state of partial undress was still going on. He was unable to determine how long he remained there. When he later recalled the moment of horror and illumination, all he remembered was glancing away from the mirror and then quickly down at his body—which he had trained himself not to look at—at the darkened area beneath his undergarment, knowing that this was the symbolic origin of the mark on his breast.

He shuddered as he covered his body, left the bathing closet, and returned to the confines of his own chamber, relieved that no one appeared to be about. But once he had returned to his room and closed the door behind him, he was confronted with a greater worry since there was no mirror in his own room for him to use if he wanted to reexamine his chest. He ripped off his nightshirt and looked down at his chest, horrified to discover that the mark was still there, looking even darker than it had appeared before. He trembled and sat down on his bed, naked, more consciously aware of his body than he had been for many years.

He glanced at the *A*, momentarily believing it was not actually the letter *A*, but some cryptic design of accident, since from the perspective of looking down at it, below his chin, it was somewhat distorted. Perhaps it was not an *A* but something else, but how was he to determine? Should he cover himself and run back into the garderobe and look into the mirror a second time? How would he know, how would he be able to keep check on any development or change—especially if, as he hoped, it was only a temporary rash and would pass away?

He looked again at his body, at the translucent flesh, that had always frightened him; examined it carefully for the first time in years, as if it were something totally foreign to him. A plethora of conflicting emotions threatened to overtake him—positive and negative feelings of repulsion and, yes, pleasure. He reached into his undergarment and touched the organ between his legs, pulled it away from his body, and examined it as if it belonged to someone else. It was more an object lesson in human anatomy than a feeling of rapture. When he released the tube of flesh, it flopped back to the space between his legs where it resumed its shrunken state. Then he ran his hands over his legs and thighs, the lower portions of his body, as if he doubted their corporeality, but again there was no moment of arousal, for his body, he concluded, had been permitted to die.

Except for the letter on his breast.

Later—years later if one measured time by the isolated epiphanies of one's life, but only minutes by the clock—Arthur heard a noise coming from somewhere in the house, and though he immediately froze on his bed, the fear of discovery in his nakedness roused him from his stupor. What if Roger Chillingworth should open the door and discover him naked, sitting on his bed? Quickly he dressed for the day, glancing at the clock over the fireplace, surprised to notice that it was still only late morning, barely past eleven o'clock.

When he was finally presentable, he listened again for sounds from the rest of the house, trying to determine who had returned: the Widow Kellings? Roger Chillingworth? But there was nothing to indicate that anyone else was in the domicile: only silence, though Arthur was certain that he had heard something before. Then he was struck by another fear, and he moved his hand to his chest, as if by doing so he could feel the scarlet letter through the folds of his cassock. There was a knock on his door, and in that moment when Arthur touched his breast and hovered on the porches of insanity, he knew that the source of the letter on his flesh had something to do with Roger Chillingworth and the old man's presence in his room during the middle of the night.

"Just a moment," Arthur replied, his voice panic-stricken as he crossed the room and grasped hold of the door.

To his relief, the figure framed in the doorway was not Roger Chillingworth or the Widow Kellings, but one of the boys from his parish, obviously embarrassed that he had entered the house without anyone letting him in. Arthur recognized him at once, a likable enough lad, though reputed to be somewhat dull-witted.

"Reverend Wilson would like to see you at the church," the boy informed him, looking past Arthur into the room.

"Tell him I will be there in a few minutes," Arthur replied, patting the boy on the head.

"I knocked at the door, but no one answered," the lad explained, by way of an apology for his entry into the house.

"Do not worry. I did not hear you. You did what you should have," Arthur answered, trying to make the boy more comfortable. "Run along now and tell Reverend Wilson that I will be there shortly. Tell him I have been ill," and he placed his hand over his chest, as if that would be sufficient explanation for the boy.

During the ensuing days, Arthur felt that he was on the verge of a mental collapse. The obsession of the past (the fear of being identified as Hester Prynne's lover) had clearly manifested itself physically upon his body in the form of the letter *A* on his breast. What had been limited to an uncontrollable obsession—guilt, fear of discovery, mental agony—had now manifested itself on his physical person. He was haunted by the letter on his bosom. How did it get there? How long had it been there? Was it simply a matter of Roger Chillingworth's necromancy? Though he feared the probing nature of the old physician's questions, he suspected it was more likely that the *A* had been on his breast for a lengthy period of time. How long, he could not be certain since his practice of avoiding any examination of his flesh meant that the *A* could have appeared there long ago without his apparent knowledge.

He lived in constant fear of discovery—of the *A* on his breast that would announce to all the world his secret crime. If Roger Chillingworth was not responsible for its appearance, had he observed it there the night he prowled around his room and tried to remove his nightshirt? If he had not observed it, what could he do to make certain that some other night when he was asleep and not feigning slumber the old man would not examine his bosom? Arthur took to moving a chair in front of the door after he closed it for the night, or even during the daytime whenever he feared the unexpected entry of the older man. Sometimes he even placed an empty pitcher on the chair—precariously balanced so it would fall to the floor if the door were opened. The result of all these anxieties wrecked havoc on his body; the nights of supposed sleep were reduced to lengthy bouts of sleeplessness, his body demanding the sleep he clearly needed, his mind refusing to shut off for fear that something would happen during the periods of slumber.

There were days when Arthur looked down at his breast and imagined that the *A* was becoming fainter, less visible, perhaps even slowly disappearing, yet whenever he examined himself in the mirror in the bathing closet, the letter stared back at him like some evil personification of his soul. He imagined the roots of the letter, grasping deep into his heart. Sometimes it looked like a face, distorted to be sure, about to talk back at him and curse him for his duplicity. Above all, Arthur was obsessed with discovering some other source of reflection so he could keep check on the progress of the letter over his heart. He polished a silver tankard he kept in his room for drinking, since it offered a possible source of reflection, but the curve of the flask only led to greater distortion, changing the shape of any object mirrored in it. Sometimes he tried to examine his chest by standing in front of the glass in one of the windows of his room, but that was a delicate business, since he could be observed by anyone below and that might lead to even greater misunderstandings. He considered purchasing a small mirror from one of the sellers in the market, but feared their questions and, worse, the rumors they might spread about his vanity. In short, it had become almost impossible to monitor the progress of the *A* on his breast except for the steady burning sensation that served as a ubiquitous reminder of its presence.

Weeks passed, then months. Arthur worried about every aspect of his life. Would he never again see Hester alone? How long could he continue his hypocritical relationship with his parishioners? What was to prevent him from babbling out his secret in the middle of his sermon: "I am the biggest sinner of them all?" He was troubled by the parasitic relationship that old Roger Chillingworth insisted upon, always probing, asking additional questions about his health—always searching for the deeper recesses of his illness. He hated his accommodations with the Widow Kellings, especially the view from the window of his room; the nearby graveyard with its ominous implications. And he hated himself, loathed his body and soul—even the sickening tone of his own voice, as if it were something to which he had become oversensitive. In short, he would have welcomed death, had that not become an even larger terror, since he knew he was damned for eternity. As awful as his life had become, death would be even worse.

The sleeplessness continued, bringing with it increased consternation. There were times when he carried on lengthy dialogues with himself and with Hester; there were moments when he could not reconcile the images that cluttered his brain—especially in the middle of the night when he lay on his bed, drenched from the persistent fever, half conscious of the most insignificant movement of his body, the slightest noise coming from outside his room or the house, halfway toward the release that sleep rarely ever brought.

"You have to help me find a key for the door, Hester. I have to have some way of locking the others out."

"Who?" Hester asked him.

"The people who wander through my room every night. They come when I am asleep, so they will not think I notice them, but I do. I know they come here. I know they watch me, even if they think I am not aware. But a key for the door would prevent all that, do you not understand?"

"A key can lock things in as well as lock things out, Arthur. Bolting the door—that is not something you can do so lightly, without thinking of the implications of what you have done."

"But I will not use it all the time—just at night so that no one will watch me, so that I can sleep without their eyes examining me."

"If you know that they are watching you, then you do not need a key, Arthur. You have mastered half of the problem by recognizing it. Tell them to leave. A key can be misused, Arthur. It can cut you off from others; it can lock you away."

"But it is not just people, Hester. I need that key for other reasons—to lock away the secrets of my soul, safely, so that no one will ever discover them. Once they are locked up like that, we will be safe, do you not see? No one will ever know. It is for your benefit also. You have got to buy a key for me and a lock."

"Why can you not buy one for yourself? No one should ever buy a key for someone else. That is not right, Arthur."

"I am too well known. I cannot go into the market and buy a lock like that. People would know right away and say that I am hiding some secret from them. You have got to do it for me; there is no one else. Maybe you could steal one. Can you not at least try, when no one is watching?"

"I will try, Arthur, but you are asking for something that is very difficult. It is the wrong way to do things."

He closed the door behind him, and motioned for Hester to sit down on a chair, but when she began to sit in the one near the door he prevented her from doing so, "No, use the other one." He pushed the chair she had been about to sit upon in front of the door so no one would be able to enter the room. "It is safer this way."

Then he took the package she had brought him and excitedly unwrapped it, like a child tearing off the paper from a birthday present. He removed the key and smiled for the first time in months, though he was smiling at the key and not at Hester. He walked back to the door and held the key close to the keyhole, without testing it, obviously satisfied with the likeness, and determined that it would fit.

He crossed over to his cupboard and pulled open the third drawer, then rummaged around until he located what he wanted—clearly pleased with his discovery—a tiny mirror he had hidden in his clothing. He held it in his left hand and with the other took the key and placed it on top of the mirror, watching the reflection instead of the key. Then he looked up from his hands and smiled at Hester.

He walked over to where she was sitting, her mouth open a half an inch or so in amazement as she watched his pantomime with the key. When she said nothing, responded in no way, he separated the key from the mirror, raised it with his right hand, and placed it into the opening between her lips.

Chapter Seven

"**D**EATH" Roger Chillingworth questioned. "You ask me about death—after all the sermons you have delivered on the subject?"

"You know that I am not a well man," Arthur responded. "I feel that all my sermons have been but faint preparation for my own life, which I can in no way control."

It was a late autumnal afternoon, and Arthur Dimmesdale had endured the probing questions of the old physician—a further attempt to discover the source of Arthur's delirium, his continued disabilities.

"I have told you, there is no physical explanation for your malady. I have examined the patient and pronounced him physically fit." He referred to Arthur in the third person, as if he were reporting his findings to some lay body of interested citizens. "And yet, this is not to suggest that the illness is not real—without a source—albeit one that is invisible. Are you certain you have told me everything that has significance upon your case?"

"I have told you a hundred times, there is nothing more to relate." Arthur shifted his weight uncomfortably on the bed where he had been sitting. The older man—seated on a chair near a window—sat rigidly on the hard wood, barely moving a muscle, though they had been together for nearly an hour.

"You must try to remember. Some incident from your youth, perhaps—an episode from the past may have bearing here. It need not be a recent event; our minds are capable of playing strange tricks with the past and letting it dominate our lives in the present. Methinks the source of your perturbation lies somewhat deeper, a misunderstood incident from your youth, perhaps. If you fail to purge yourself of this cancer, it will hold you down until the end.''

"All I need is some medicine to free me of this blight, but the remedy you offer is unlike the kind other doctors give their patients. What kind of healer is that?''

"Not a healer of men's souls, my friend,'' the older man replied. "That is your domain.''

"Not a healer of men's bodies either,'' Arthur responded.

"Oh, that is the easy part—though not for you. What I offer instead is what I learned from my tenure with the Indians—the world of incantations and spirits, good and bad, reduplicated in our troubled minds.''

"But that is blasphemy,'' Arthur was quick to respond.

"No more than the irreverence of your own world with its Devil worship. What I offer you is belief in yourself—a kind of emotional purity—if the patient will but try to heal himself.''

"My church offers much the same—faith and spiritual purity for the troubled body, if we give ourselves entirely to our Maker.''

"But the minister does not appear to be able to heal himself. His flock, yes, where his success has never been counted greater. Would that not make an interesting revelation to his many followers—the savior who cannot ransom himself?''

"I fear what my parishioners fear the same as they: sin, the Devil's temptations, death. These aversions hold me down as they do the members of my flock, reminding me daily that I am no better than anyone else.''

"But I thought you were one of God's elect, good Reverend Dimmesdale, ah, a Visible Saint, assured the riches of heaven, the powers of the universe—everlasting life.''

"Even a Visible Saint has fears and doubts. If God's determined but once stopped believing in the inevitability of their election, sin would be rampant and chaos would prevail. The Devil would win in his campaign against God's goodness. There would be no order in men's lives. Each man would stand alone.''

"But is that not your condition at this very moment, Reverend Dimmesdale? Have you not by your own fears cast yourself off from the people around you? Their lives are ordered and simple—a part of the collective whole. They tell you their petty sins and weaknesses—and perhaps even now and then one of genuine disorder—but by their confessions they are cleansed of their inner turmoil. But you, by contrast, by the fears instilled by your very church, you are a man standing alone. Is that what the Puritan elect see as their mission in New England, that each man will finally stand deserted in his dread?''

"Were you not a Christian once yourself?" Arthur asked the older man.

"Yes, indeed, until my recent life among the heathen peoples, whom you would try to convert to your superior ways so that they in time will endure the same sophisticated obsessions from which you suffer.''

Arthur could make no response to the older man's troubling statements. He shifted his position on his bed the better to look outside the window of his room. But even there—in the many gravestones that jutted out so rigidly from the ground—there was no remedy for his tortured soul.

"You see that headstone there?" Roger Chillingworth began, the suddenness of the alteration in his discourse surprising Arthur. He pointed at one of the tombstones in the distance.

"Which one?" Arthur moved more closely to the edge of his bed.

"Hannah Grey's—the third one in the row after the stepping-stones. Look closely at your faith recorded in stone, the perfect subject for one of your sermons: death's configuration made real for even the strongest doubter. How fitting that even there—in your Christian cemetery—the final hour should shine so horrifically. The skull at the top of Hannah Grey's tombstone, a reminder to all of the horror of death. The sunken eyes, the cleft nose, the bared teeth, certainly in no way an indication of happiness or even relief as death should be, but, rather, the wages of Hell. The cavern Hannah Grey was buried in leads straight to the flames of Hades, and lest you doubt it, look at the figurations in the stone. Even the hourglass under the skull—you think it was carved there for mere ornamentation? Those wings, removed from the skull, foretelling no possible flight for poor Mistress Grey. Never will her soul soar into the heavens. Methinks those wings even look as if they weigh her down, hold her more firmly to the fires of the inferno. There is no exit. No escape. What think you of your religion now, good Reverend?''

"You see what you want to see," Arthur responded, without looking at the tombstone in question. "I look at that graveyard and see signs of freedom and solace, relief from this troubled land. You see, instead, the Devil's works where others vision only a greater heaven.''

"Do you really? Are you certain?" the physician asked him. "Do you think that that is what death will finally bring you?"

Arthur closed his eyes, held them so tightly he could feel them burning in their sockets, and then whispered a nearly inaudible "No."

"Aha! So I thought. That is the iconography of your religion, and yet you accuse me of Devil worship, of participating in unnatural incantations with the heathens, those living artifacts of the past who daily attest to the Devil's power over New England."

"You have lived among those Devils, and yet you still speak in jest?" Arthur retorted, attempting to marshal his thoughts to the defensive.

"Ah, yes, the usual line of primitive logic sanctioned by the church: the Indians are heathens, thus handmaidens of the Devil. Save an Indian—convert him to Puritanism—and you save not only his soul but by your good works you will save your own. Ergo, any man who is held in captivity by the Indians is being punished for his sins. I am the man who lived among Indians; therefore, I lived with the Devil. Perhaps I even *am* the Devil. A simple dialectic; an example of Christian logic." When Arthur made no response, the older man continued. "Do you follow me? I know you do. My captivity, you believe, was punishment for my sin, a journey into Hell—never mind what my sin was. We will answer that some other time. I was being punished, or—if you will—my faith was being tested by God when he threw me to those wild Indians. After all, captivity, like all our lesser trials, is only a manifestation of God's providence, though in this case one I would hardly care to recommend for the rest of our foul race."

Arthur cleared his throat, tried to speak, but no words would come forth. He sat on his bed in a position which suggested that he had been thrown there by some superior force, afraid to look Roger Chillingworth directly in the face, yet unable to stop listening to his discourse.

"You remain silent, Reverend Dimmesdale. Let me continue. God punished me for my sins when he threw me into the hands of the Natives. But, as you can see, I survived, I lived to tell the tale. I returned from the world of the dead. My survival, then, has certified God's favor, my redemption. *I am one of the elect*—not you, poor soul, with all your doubts and fears." He stopped talking for a minute, then continued: "But you question even this, so let me show you proof of my season in Hell—a little picture of what you have yet in store. Here, let me use that candle.'' He pointed to Arthur's dresser and the candleholder that sat there upon.

Arthur slowly rose from the bed, walked over to the dresser, and removed the candleholder. He handed it to the older man, puzzled because though dusk was approaching, the outside was still bathed in the final rays of sunlight.

''Do you have a tinder-box?'' Roger Chillingworth asked him.

Instead of replying to his question, Arthur returned to his dresser and removed the desired object from the top drawer.

''Now bring it here,'' the older man commanded, as if he were talking to a small child, ''and I will demonstrate the wonders of the unseen world.''

Arthur handed him the tinder-box, then watched the older man light the candle and hold it out between them. ''Give me your hand for a moment.'' Before Arthur realized what had happened, the leech had grabbed his hand and forced it into the flame.

Arthur let out a scream, pulling away from the older man. ''Madman, is that how you cure your patients?'' There was fire in Arthur's eyes, as instinctively he placed the burned finger in his mouth.

''Never fear, you will suffer no harm. By tomorrow it will no longer burden you. Would that I could heal your other malady as easily.'' Roger Chillingworth returned to the chair he had been sitting in earlier, the candle still flickering in his hand.

''Now tell me, my good man, how long do you think your flesh endured the flame from this candle?'' When there was no reply from the younger man, Roger Chillingworth continued, ''Five seconds? Ten? More than that?''

Arthur shook his head, still nursing the pain in his finger. He had returned to his former position on the bed but kept his eyes on the older man in case he tried to surprise him with another one of his tricks.

''Can we agree upon it, then, no more than ten seconds?''

''Less than that. Less than five. A second or two at most. And you think that you can give that as your example of Hell—where the flames are eternal? You think that little preview is all I need for a fear of Hell?'' He stopped nursing his finger, as if to prove to the older man that he was no longer in pain.

''Would that our life were that simple. Now watch and listen as I count away the seconds.'' The older man paused, and Arthur observed him place his left palm over the flame of the candle.

Arthur held his breath, expecting his companion to cry out in pain. And then to his sudden surprise, for he had already forgotten the second part of Roger Chillingworth's pronouncement, he heard the older man begin to count off the seconds: "One. Two. Three. Four. Five. . . ." And the voice droned on, slowly and steadily at a slower pace than Arthur knew a clock would measure the time. "Eighteen. Nineteen. Twenty. Twenty-one," the leech continued.

The flame flickered unevenly, yet Roger Chillingworth's hands—one holding the candle, the other in the flame—remained steady, and with no visible trembling at all. "Thirty-five. Thirty-six. Thirty-seven. . . ."

Arthur gritted his teeth and held his breath, spellbound by the old man's self-inflicted torture. By the time he had reached the early fifties, the room was filled with a sickening odor of burning flesh; and Arthur knew, if the older man did not stop this beastly act, that he, Arthur, would faint.

"Fifty-six. Fifty-seven. Fifty-eight. Fifty-nine. Sixty. One minute. Should I continue?" Still, there was no mark of pain on the physician's face, nor any vibration. His hand remained consumed by the pale blue flame.

When Arthur failed to respond, the physician began again: "One. Two. Three. Four. . . ."

"Enough!" Arthur screamed, leaping from his bed and knocking the candle to the floor. He jumped up and down upon it, trampling it into the hardwood floor, as if by this act he could release the stifled rage deep within his person.

Roger Chillingworth returned to his chair. The younger man noticed that the older one made no attempt to nurse the hand that had been burned; no attempt even to exercise the fingers. His hand remained at his side as if nothing were wrong with it. Arthur stood before his bed, unable to make a decision whether to sit back down. Then he spoke, "So what do you want to prove—that one of us is insane?"

"Oh, that it were as simple a matter as insanity, Arthur," the leech replied, for the first time in Arthur's memory calling him by his Christian name. "That was a little exercise in tolerance, or possibly we should call it intolerance."

Arthur remained silent, blushing, waiting for his companion to continue. "You think you know what hell I endured among those savages? What you saw just now with that candle was nothing by comparison. Speak to me not of pain, brother, unless you know of what you speak. You—who cannot even endure the candle's flame for a second. Let me tell you now about my life among the savages, my life with the devils."

He paused, but Arthur made no attempt to spur him on. He simply waited to hear what the older man would say. Roger Chillingworth settled himself a little more comfortably in his chair, still paying no attention to his scorched flesh. Outside it was fast approaching darkness, and Arthur wondered if he dare light another candle.

"Our ship was thrown off course, blown far north by spring storms, and we arrived not here on your eastern coastal lands but north at an unsettled area of the New-found-land, home of the Beothic Indians. Had the captain known of the troubles we would encounter, he would never have tried to ditch the vessel where he did, but we had been too long at sea—the ship damaged beyond repair—all of us broken by the long voyage. In short, it was an ill move—the ship cracked apart on the rocks, but five of us survived—myself and four of the crew. The sailors swam ashore, after pulling off their clothing; I held on to a wooden chest and was washed to the beach. There I arrived, a proper gentleman, still dressed in my city clothes—the others quite naked as the day they were born.

"Our greeting? Who met us? A group of ravaging Beothic, who immediately set upon my companions and chopped them to pieces before my eyes, within minutes after my safe harbor from the sea. My own survival I can only attribute to the oddity of my garments, to some unusual attraction in my dress. Perhaps the Beothic thought I was a creature from the sea, some god or goddess dressed in curious garments. My companions were recognized immediately by their nakedness as mere mortals and thus murdered.

"I closed my eyes, waiting what was certainly my own predetermined fate, when to my surprise I felt a dozen or more hands touching me, feeling my clothing, struggling with my appearance and trying to reconcile it with their own. I feared it would only be a matter of seconds before my garments would be ripped from my body and there I would stand in my nakedness, like their own, and I too would be identified like the others as a mere mortal man. I tried to struggle against their probing fingers, to keep my identity a secret, when all at once I was saved by a miracle of our civilization: my pocket watch.

"It was a purely fortuitous accident, for I had carefully placed my watch in my trousers, connected by the fob, shortly before the call to abandon ship and it had somehow remained attached to my person, still ticking away what I could only foresee were the final moments of my life. What prevented the watch from becoming waterlogged, I do not know. But I must digress for a minute and tell you something about that watch.''

Arthur looked at Roger Chillingworth who had remained immobile on his chair. The room had become so opaque, it was almost impossible to see the older man's expression, and the idea passed through his mind that his companion might be fabricating the entire tale, sneering at him as he spun it out, like thread from the spinnerets of an arachnid.

"The watch—which I no longer possess—had one identifying characteristic which distinguished it from all others I have ever seen: an alarm which could be set—like much larger clocks—so that it would ring at a predetermined time. I had carried it since the beginning of my medical practice. No doubt the watch itself would have been sufficient to startle those hungry hands that were probing at my body, but without the alarm they would have massacred me like my companions before the discovery of the precious object. Instead, in the general mêlée, the alarm went off, frightening the Indians who groped at my body as if it were so many tattered garments thrown to a ragpicker.

"The alarm went off, I say, and the savages jumped back in surprise, permitting me a moment to collect my thoughts. I removed the valuable object from my pocket and held it up for everyone to see, quickly winding it in case I suddenly needed to rely on its unusual sound during another onslaught from those savages. At first they were frightened, but I by so many signs pointed to the sea and then at myself and the timepiece to indicate that both of us had come from some more powerful being. Soon, one or two of the braver savages came close enough to observe the mysterious object—which I would not relinquish to their greedy hands, but instead held to their ears so they could listen to the life within the shiny, perplexing case. Shortly, by indications that I could understand, I was told to follow them away from the beach and into the forest, where I guessed they had set up their camp.''

Roger Chillingworth paused for a minute to catch his breath, perhaps to organize his thoughts—in the darkness, it was difficult for Arthur to tell. When no sound was forthcoming from the older man's voice, a sudden chill came over the younger man, frightened by the leech's presence in the nearly darkened room. Then the physician's voice broke the silence:

"Let me describe to you what happened in that Indian camp, my confinement in the underworld. Clearly, the watch had saved me, but for how long I could not say. I had witnessed four of my shipmates chopped down like so many blades of grass, and I lived in constant fear that a similar fate lay in store for me. The chief of the Beothic Indians, to whom I was taken, took even more interest in my watch than had his underlings, regarding it as his property, his private fetish—insisting from the start that it remain in his care and not in mine. Meanwhile, I became his personal servant, my immediate worry being that I could not remain in those foolish garments of mine forever without my corporeal existence so identified as like their own.

"I lived, ate, slept in the chief's lodge, daily watching my garments wear thin and, even more upsetting, fearing the hour the watch would stop beating, for I knew that it was being overtaxed by their cunning leader who persisted in making the alarm go off at all hours of the day. The period arrived—sooner than I had feared—when the timepiece simply stopped, both its alarm and its ticking in the same day, and though I took it apart and carefully tried to restore it to its former function, it was to no avail. It had simply given up the ghost as I feared my own life shortly would.

"The function of the watch eliminated—that of my faithful totem—my relationship with the chief was suddenly altered. Thus began a series of experiments to determine if I was, in fact, a god or mortal man, trials which I knew full well would determine my survival or my death. Three days after the sudden demise of the watch, I noticed the chief talking secretly with his advisors, huddled together in fast dialogue in low tones as if they feared I could understand their language. That night, when food was prepared for the others and brought to them for their daily meal, I noticed that no one had bothered to bring a bowl for me, though everyone was looking in my direction. Then, shortly, one of the chief's wives brought me a bowl of human excrement and placed it on the ground before me. I was told to eat what was in the bowl. Of course, I immediately refused, indicating that I was not hungry.

"This process continued for several days, as my hunger increased ravenously and I feared I would die from starvation. Though I nibbled away at grass and roots when no one was about, my hunger soon brought delirium I knew it would be impossible to control. On the sixth night, I was instructed in no uncertain terms to eat the contents of the bowl, which I did in such a stupor that my nausea was somehow controlled until such time, later that night, when I was able to force my fingers down my throat and expel the putrid repast.''

Arthur thought that his own stomach was about to retch. He wanted to scream out for the older man to stop his discourse but was afraid he would be laughed at, since his ordeal was merely to listen to what Roger Chillingworth had endured. Sensing the abhorrence in the younger man on the bed, the physician continued:

''You have heard enough, perhaps?'' he asked, emitting a hurried little laugh, ''Ah, no. That was just the beginning. For water I was given urine; for food, excrement and all matter of even fouler matter. All of which I drank and ate, consuming with much fury at times to prove to those savages that I was not a mortal man as they. For certain, I would not be here to tell you this were it not for the pity that one of the chief's own wives bestowed upon me, hiding food and water for me in such places where I could consume them without fear of discovery. I mention that old woman for one reason only—not because she saved my life, but because she showed me that even there, in the perversity of that defiled clutch of heathen people, one human being identified with another and established an everlasting bond.

''What I was shortly to discover was that old Mytobie, that old woman as she was called, had been kicked around by the chief, treated as his dog for so many years that her own humanity, which should have been in question, took its natural course. She sided with me, now clearly the underdog who had usurped her place as scapegoat or whipping boy for the others. I lived in dread fear that her ministrations would be discovered and my diet shortly altered.

''I lost track of time. Days became weeks, perhaps months. There was no way to tell. My body was on the verge of collapse, my garments hung loose on me; I was sick from the strange course of my daily intake of nourishment. Even worse, winter was shortly upon us and I feared the bitter cold would add to my general deterioration. Yet there I remained in the chief's lodge, trying to keep my illnesses a secret from the others, a demonstration of my comfort and stability. How long I ate that disgusting food I cannot be certain, but one night I discovered in my bowl the same repast as the others, and though I immediately suspected some new trick at play, I shortly learned from Mytobie that I had won the first round with the chief. I had survived his enforced diet; there seemed to be no reason for him to continue with the same rigidity. Besides, I suspect I had become a health problem for the others.''

Arthur could stand it no longer—the disembodied voice

resonating throughout his chamber in the darkness. When Roger Chillingworth paused, Arthur informed him that he was going to light another candle. "No tricks this time, understand," and he got up from his bed and lit a fresh candle. He was surprised to see the older man sitting in his chair, as if in a trance, his rheumy eyes closed as if the light from the candle would blind him. Arthur returned to his bed.

"Instead, there were new tests of endurance for me," Roger Chillingworth continued, his eyes still closed. "There was a small boy, perhaps three or four years old, in the chief's lodge—one of his many grandchildren but clearly his favorite—who was often given the task of lighting his grandfather's pipe of an evening after the daily meal. I had noticed this child many times before, precariously—yet skillfully—balancing a live coal he had removed from the campfire with two sticks and carry it over to his grandfather so the old chief could light his pipe. It was an innocent if not a ritualistic matter, the child only the catalyst for what happened.

"One night just before the old man was going to light his pipe— after the boy had brought the burning ember—he pulled the pipe away from his grandson, forcing the coal to fall to the ground. The child laughed—a matter that surprised me since these people rarely expressed any spontaneous emotions. Then he bent over with his sticks and was about to pick up the coal when his grandfather signaled for me to come over to his side. I suspected some foul play but, knowing my options, walked slowly toward him. He pointed to the burning object, indicating that I should pick it up so that he could light his pipe. When I attempted to take the sticks from the child's hands, the chief quickly grabbed them and broke them in two. Then he indicated a second time that I was to pick up the smoldering coal and place it in his pipe.

"That was only the beginning. I held my breath and with a movement as fast as possible grabbed hold of the coal and put it in the chief's pipe. Since it had been removed from the fire some minutes earlier, I did not burn my fingers badly. That plus the fact that I had only to lift it a few feet. But the chief could not get his pipe to light—or so he informed me—and instructed me to bring another coal from the open fire. I knew I would be burned, of course, the distance from the hearth to the old man being rather considerable, plus the fact that I would be holding a coal that was much more intense in its temperature."

Roger Chillingworth paused and opened his eyes for a moment as if to glance at Arthur and note the expression on his face. Then he continued, before the younger man was offered the chance to respond.

"I did it, of course—not just once, but a hundred times, night after night—for the chief and all his lesser functionaries who suddenly had taken a liking to smoking their pipes after dark. Not once did I cry out from the pain that I endured, from the scorched and singed fingers, the skin of which fell off in soft, leprous pieces after each act of bringing fire to those beastly savages. I even learned the best way to carry a white-hot coal so that only a portion of my hand would be burned, perfected a way of doing the impossible. It was either that or immediate death, though I knew it would only be a matter of time before my torturers would devise some sacrificial death for me, again to test my mortality.

"You understand, now, how I tricked you into observing my object lesson with the candle. My flesh burned, for you smelled it and can smell it even now. Of course, I felt the pain from that flame, but I was able to endure it as you and others cannot. For I have walked through hell and survived, while you, my friend, still stand at the gateway, your journey into the future made paltry by an inner misery that eats your flesh even now as you listen to my wild discourse."

Again, Arthur was not certain how he was to respond to Roger Chillingworth's prognostications. He felt as if he had been listening to the older man's dialogue for hours, but knew also that the physician's story was far from completed. There was still some missing episode—if nothing else the explanation for the older man's presence in his chamber. He glanced at Roger Chillingworth's face—furrowed with wrinkles, still darkened by the elements, half in shadow because of the position of the candle.

"It is true that I fear death," Arthur muttered, rather quietly, "more than you will ever know. I fear it closing in upon me every hour of the day and night and know that there is nothing that I can do to postpone it. But if, as you say, you fear it not—because nothing can rival the terrors you have already encountered upon this earth—if that be so, I beg you, as my physical protector, help me understand this imminent darkness that reaches out and threatens to surround me even now."

"We have spoken directly on that matter to no avail. You have only to unburden your heart of whatever disturbs you and this agony will pass away. You suffer from no physical malady, Reverend Dimmesdale. Your fears are of an inner kind, hinged to some significant event in your past." He raised his voice and opened his eyes. "Try to remember the source of this discomfort."

"Is there no other way?" Arthur pleaded, aware of the paltriness of his voice.

"Yes, there is another way also, but its application will not work for you."

"Tell me!"

"I have already hinted at that too; it was the purpose of my interrupted narrative. You can eliminate this fear by renouncing what you are."

"My ministry?" Arthur questioned.

"More than that: by renouncing your affiliation to a religion that places the Devil second only to its Godhead. Do you not see, dear man, that the belief in the former assumes the corruption of the latter?"

"Yet you yourself admitted that you have survived a season in Hell."

"That was a mere figure of speech. The hell that I walked through was man-made, not God-made. Can you not understand the difference?"

"How, then, can you speak of your torturers as anything but savages, antithetical to civilization—butchers, the Devil's handiwork—living examples of man's need for spiritual enlightenment?"

"Do you not remember what I told you about Mytobie and the aid she gave me when I would certainly have perished from lack of proper nourishment and continued abuse?"

"But she was regarded as a beast by the others. And even for you, she was nothing more than an enlightened animal."

"So are we all. That is all we can strive to be."

"Nonsense. You cannot distort actuality like that. One savage, one simple creature, among all your torturers aided you in your survival. One out of many, and yet you attempt to connect old Mytobie with the denizens of this covenant—or any other community in God's firmament. Your argument is riddled with holes."

"You have yet to hear the remainder of my story, Reverend Dimmesdale. I was not rescued by white men. I do not sit here today because of my faith in the lighter races."

"Continue, by all means," Arthur responded, making a rather limp gesture with his right hand, which suddenly reminded him of the finger that had been burned by the candle. Somehow, it no longer appeared to bother him. When he felt it carefully, there seemed to be no evidence that it had ever been burned in the first place.

"As you have clearly guessed, I would not be here today if the Beothic Indians had had any say in the matter. My death was the only certainty as far as they were concerned. There is no way to determine what wickedness lay in store for me, as subject of their next experiment, once I had demonstrated my skills as a carrier of fire." He paused and Arthur thought he detected a limpid chuckle.

"Is that what I was? Yes, a fire carrier. The man who brought fire to the Beothic. I have never thought of it that way before. Is there not some myth about the man who stole fire from the gods?"

"Prometheus," Arthur replied.

"Ah, yes, I had forgotten. Anyway, my days I knew were surely numbered, but then suddenly all was altered—in the period of a single night. But I must go back a step by reason of explanation so you do not regard this as some deus ex machina.

"I was not the only prisoner held by those savage people. There were others, though I was the only white man. The others—three in number—were Indians from neighboring tribes, captives of warfare. Two of them, I learned, were women, used as domestic slaves and concubines. They had been captured a year or so before, and already were sufficiently pacified, offering little threat to the subjugators. New-found-land offers a remarkable advantage to the Beothic, since there was hardly any probability of those two women stealing a canoe and fleeing to the mainland to obtain their freedom.

"The third captive, however, was a man of respect even among the Beothic, since he possessed those powers of a priestdoctor and served in that capacity to the chief and his retinue. His name as we would say it in English was Darkleaf, and he was a Penobscot who had lived for four seasons with the Beothic, healing the sick and the infirm by his diverse talents. During the course of his stay, he had earned the respect of the elders who permitted him a modicum of freedom to search in the woods for such berries and plants as he needed for the implementation of his cures. I knew of his identity because he had attempted to aid me when I suffered from the acute discomfort of dysentery, but the chief had not permitted his assistance. What I did not know, until later, was that he was an outsider who had spent every hour of his captivity devising a plan for his escape.

"Since I have no exact recollection of the months I spent in captivity, except for the passing of the seasons, I can only guess that our escape took place nine or ten months after my captivity began, sometime during the spring. Because Darkleaf had planned the entire escape, and he—more than I—was aware of the difficulties of attempting to flee during the brutal winter, I conclude that it must have been May or June. The ice was largely gone, the camp had opened up for the spring fishing season, and those endless days of confinement to the lodge that typified the dreadful winter had come to an end.

"What is remarkable to me, even today, is that in retrospect our escape appears so simple, as if it involved no complications at all. What I remember is that it had been another spring day when it was raining, when the outer gloom threatened to permeate even the fire in our lodge. Fortunately, I did not even know that the possibility of escape was in store for me, since Darkleaf and I had never had any direct communication except for his singular attempt to cure me of my dysentery. All I knew was that during the early hours of the evening, my captors appeared to be exceptionally tired, yawning loudly and falling asleep at an unquestionably earlier hour than usual. Wives, children, warriors—even the dogs—seemed to be overtaken by some powerful agent of slumber. Ha! Indeed they were, for Darkleaf had drugged them to the lot by placing a narcotic in their food. Even today, I do not know how my own bowl was free of that powerful sleeping agent." He stopped abruptly and asked the younger man, "You are tired of listening to my story? Should I continue this some other time?"

"No, go on. Just let me light another candle." Arthur did as he said, saving the stub from the earlier one for later remelting.

"In the middle of the night, I was suddenly awakened by a hand over my mouth so that I would not cry out, and a steady pull at my shoulder. At first, I thought my final hours had arrived, and I cringed at the sudden jolt to my system. But then in a moment all was apparent when from the remaining coals in the fire I could see the drugged bodies lying in unnatural positions and identified the chief's own medicine man as my deliverer.

"Carefully, we made our way out of the lodge, climbing over the sprawled bodies that lay in all manner of unusual extensions. When we reached the entrance to the lodge, I could identify nothing at all in the darkness that enveloped the outside world. I felt a faint mist falling, and in my fear of the discovery of our sudden flight, I held on to Darkleaf's arm with all my might.

"It was no easy escape in that murky darkness, the ground sodden from spring rains and melting snow. I was cold, my garments soon wet throughout, my body weakened from the repeated bouts with dysentery and my work as fire carrier. More than once I fell upon the ground and would have all but given up in my flight for freedom were it not for Darkleaf's constant attentions. When I was too weak to continue, he lifted me, pulled me by his side with some uncanny force as if he had the power of half a dozen men his size. There were no shoes or moccasins on my feet, since I had been forbidden to wear those clever objects, for fear, no doubt, that I would try to escape. Yet we ran over earth and stone, broken branches, sharp rocks, and ice till I all but concluded my flesh would shortly fall off in chunks of raw skin, as had already happened to my hands.

"When dawn finally arrived, there was hardly a change at all in the intensity of the darkness, since the fog had rolled in during the night, protecting us from further scrutiny by other Beothic on the island. By midmorning, miraculously, we had reached the area where Darkleaf had hidden a canoe for our further escape, laden down with such provisions as were necessary for our journey."

Roger Chillingworth stopped once again in his narrative to inject an element by way of explication: "You begin to understand now the course of my dialogue. Darkleaf was no savage beast; though he has not been converted to your religion, he will not be doomed to an eternity in Hell. He is not one of Lucifer's co-workers. Would that all white men were as enlightened as he. Does it make sense for us to relegate his soul to oblivion?"

Arthur made no response, the conflicts in his own mind impossible to rectify. The leech continued: "There were two fears then that dominated my weakened consciousness. First, that we would be captured again, by other Beothic of the island. And, second, that I would not survive the voyage to the mainland, to Darkleaf's people. The first was the more likely possibility, since Darkleaf was afraid to take to the open water in our small craft. Rather, we followed the rugged coast northward until it ended at the strait leading to the mainland. This was no insignificant journey, though I was delirious much of the time, unaware of the difficult days we encountered.

"During my residence with the Beothic, my body had become a storehouse of diseases. I could no longer eat solid foods. Both my hands and feet were covered with open, festering sores. But—and this is the miracle of my account—Darkleaf had brought along his medicine pouch and nursed me slowly back to health. What he cured, what he did for me would not have been possible with medicine as we know it in our world, the potions he administered being unknown to Old World physicians. Though it was no rapid event, my body inched back to safety. By the time we reached the mainland, I was no longer delirious. I could eat more normally than at anytime in months. These secrets of Indian medicine, which I subsequently learned from him, I have attempted to incorporate into my own profession—placing them often at a premium to what I learned at the university.

"Since I detect some weariness on your part, let me be brief and bring my narrative to a conclusion. As you have guessed, we finally reached Darkleaf's people safely, though not without a number of near mishaps there is no reason to describe here. Once we reached the neighboring tribes, it was easier for Darkleaf to negotiate our safe passage. By midsummer we had located his people, and I was all but recovered from my physical disabilities. Darkleaf was welcomed back home by his people as if he were some kind of warrior gloriously returned from battle, his family and friends having long given him up for lost. He immediately resumed his honored position as healer of his people, as respected member of his clan.

"I spent almost a year with Darkleaf and his people, learning the Penobscot language and such secrets of Darkleaf's medical knowledge as he would willingly impart to me. And there among those gentle people I learned a respect for the red man's ways and customs, gained a perspective for examining my own conscience and previous attitudes. From them I acquired a new respect for mankind, a greater understanding of man's obligation to his fellowmen—instead of some invisible being—appreciation for the communal whole of which each man is only a tiny, insignificant speck. If, in fact, I learned anything from my days with Darkleaf's people, it was that we Europeans are slowly severing our ties with one another, building barriers that will eventually place each of us inside a prison of our own creation, as you are even now in your refusal to expel the troubled matter from your psyche."

Roger Chillingworth looked at the younger man on the bed as if he expected his narrative to jolt him from his lethargy. Arthur ignored the remark, though his right hand advanced unconsciously to his bosom.

"My faith teaches me similarly—a sense of the bounty for one's fellowmen," Arthur said calmly.

"Your faith is a fraud!" the older man exclaimed, his voice suddenly in a rage. "It is based upon the example of moral superiority.

It sets up a hierarchy for goodness and purity, relegating whole masses of people to a future of blackness while choosing a small elite for everlasting peace and comfort. Even the very people who profess to believe in this strange division—the disenfranchised majority who are doomed forever—blindly accept these fanatical proportions, living under the misguided delusion that signs of their election will miraculously appear at the moment of their demise. You call that enlightenment?''

"Have you so easily forgotten your Beothic torturers?" Arthur asked him.

"Those tortures were mere child's play—nothing at all compared to what I have witnessed and heard of our European heritage and its endless attempts to pacify these innocent peoples. Do not speak to me of outrages against the body when you know not of the sophistications of European punishment. No culture has a monopoly on human brutality. That is the only lesson we can learn from the history of our limited stay on this earth. Now I leave you to your Maker, since my story appears to have made little effect upon you.''

They seemed to have arrived at a standoff. The older man stood up, apparently anxious to leave the room. He remained there for a minute, perhaps waiting for Arthur to make some additional response, but Arthur did not know what to say. What Roger Chillingworth was asking for was nothing less than a confession of his innermost thoughts and secrets, as if their roles had been reversed and the older man had become the minister. Arthur started to get up from the bed when Roger Chillingworth spoke again:

"You know, my friend, that yours is a sacred role—healer of man's inner soul. You can rehabilitate everyone's soul but your own. Religion is the antidote of the masses. My own lessons from Darkleaf and his people suggest that medicine is also sacred—for I, too, deal with the mind of the patient, not just with his body. My dysentery was cured by chemical agents, as were the sores on my hands and feet. But there is also a medicine of the mind that can cure visitations upon the body and the flesh which have no physical origin due to torture or accident.

"Suppose, for example, you were to awaken one morning and discover some strange disfigurement covering a portion of your body—your arms or your chest, for example—emblazoned with some wondrous mark. That configuration upon your body could be caused by some inner fear or tension, by the closing off of the personality from other human matters and concerns—perhaps the cause of some frightful embarrassment or unchecked frailty. Examine your body frequently for such imperfections, for they can overtake us when we least suspect them. Consider your body as an extension of the mind. Consider your dreams and your waking fears.''

And with those pronouncements, Roger Chillingworth left Arthur stranded upon his bed.

Chapter Eight

I<small>N</small> the months that followed Roger Chillingworth's exegesis, the young minister reached the depths of his despair. Autumn, winter, spring—each season brought with it reminders of his unresolvable dilemma, his self-enforced isolation from the world around him. The smallest incident or sign brought reminders of his fast-approaching death. Though he no longer suffered from the earlier respiratory diseases, his body continued to waste away—each day he looked more gaunt and withered. Were he not the assistant pastor of First Church, one can surmise that his ghostlike appearance would have led to speculations and even jeers that he had made an alliance with the Devil, or at least some powerful force that sucked his blood like a lamia. His cassock, which had always been loose fitting, draped about him like a sheet—a shroud, Arthur often thought—his body swimming in the excessive folds of cloth. Even his shoes, he felt, had become too large for him.

Everywhere he looked he was reminded of his sin and his greater fear of death. His aloneness—without Hester and Pearl—took its daily toll upon him, especially during the winter months when he was confined for lengthy periods to his room. There was no one to talk to but the Widow Kellings, who was approaching senility and often incoherent, and Roger Chillingworth, whom he could hear too frequently from the rest of the house, engaged in his latest medical experiments. Though their lives were necessitously interlocked—because of the proximity of their rooms—their conversation, since the night of the older man's lengthy narrative, had become increasingly formal, as Arthur—always on guard for fear of revealing the slightest clue about his relationship with Hester—became nearly monosyllabic in the older man's presence.

What had the leech discovered about him? What did those cryptic comments at the conclusion of their dialogue foretell? A thousand times Arthur thought about their portents, but still he was unable to resolve the confusion: was old Roger Chillingworth responsible for the *A* that had appeared on his bosom, or was it a manifestation of his own hidden guilt? Had the leech simply surmised that Arthur's chest was covered with a concealed disfigurement or had he—through his evil incantations—caused it to appear thereon? Why was the older man always prying into his life, probing, digging into his most private affairs? What made this man—who had expounded so eloquently upon the humanity of the Indians and the need for human compassion—such a parasite, seemingly drawing his very livelihood from the misery of others?

Arthur agonized not only because of his hidden sin but also over his wizened appearance, since he knew that others had certainly detected the changes in his physique. The Reverend John Wilson—always concerned with his assistant pastor's livelihood—had reiterated his suggestions that what Arthur most needed in life was a wife. And, in fact, more than one of the young virgins in Arthur's parish had blushed uncontrollably in his presence, suggesting their willingness to become his spouse. His influence with the youth of the church had never been at a higher period of esteem. They seemed to agonize over their pastor's gaunt appearance, which had the effect of making him appear like some romantic hero of yore, pining away from unrequited love. His holiness, his purity was the subject of the gossip of many an adolescent of his church.

The more these devoted followers showed their concern for his discomfort—recommending always closer ties with Roger Chillingworth—the more Arthur agonized at his worsened physical state. The *A* on his breast was not even the subject of his greatest concern, since its life had come to a standstill; it always appeared the same. Instead, Arthur was concerned about his face—the most visible aspect of his altered state. In the autumn, he had even made bold enough to steal a small mirror from one of the booths in the market, slipping it inside the folds of his cassock when the seller was assisting someone else. This act of petty thievery—which would have mortified him in earlier times—quickly passed him by with few twinges of the guilt that otherwise controlled his waking hours.

Arthur kept the stolen mirror hidden away in his room inside a book he had hollowed out for the purpose, increasingly substituting the mirror for his contact with the outer world. Sometimes he would sit for long hours, carefully examining the face that looked back at him with such remorseful sadness. Did it belie his hidden guilt? Would someone else observing it be able to detect that this was the face of a sinner, an adulterer—a fornicator? He feared that some strange alteration had taken over the pupils of his eyes, thereby permitting anyone who looked at him to glance deep within his soul and immediately identify him as the hypocritical monster he had become. The eyes, the lips, even the nose—all were obvious to anyone who thought for a moment about the debilitation that had made its mark on all portions of his corporeal being.

At times of his deepest morbidity—on the mornings he delivered a sermon to his congregation—he was often reduced to babbling incoherently, merely anticipating his public stance in front of his many followers. He would climb the steps leading to the pulpit, fully expecting to stand there rambling on illogically, emitting gibberish and fragments of syllables as if his body were possessed by some evil spirit—or worse, his jaws locked together by some terrible force that would make it impossible for him to open them and spew forth the pious examples his congregation had come to expect. Why had God not struck him dead in the pulpit? More than once he had climbed those dreaded steps fully intent upon preaching a full disclosure of his sins—the public confession that would lift the awful burden from his soul. More than once, when he climbed back down those steps, he had no idea at all of the subject he had preached about for the past hour and a quarter.

What was Hester to him now? And little Pearl? One spring day when Arthur sat examining his face in the mirror, he suddenly realized that he had no recollection of what Hester Prynne looked like. Her image had become a total haze. He knew the color of her hair and her eyes, of course, but he could reconstruct no composite image of her general appearance. This woman—for whom he had given his life and now his assured death—had become a nebula to him. He could not visualize her countenance any longer. Worse, he had little idea of what had happened to her life these several years since their fateful encounters.

How can this be? he asked himself. What have I become that Hester Prynne's image no longer resides in my mind—that the memory of her has already disappeared? Was her love of so little importance that she could be forgotten as easily as that? What of Pearl? That was slightly better, for Arthur could remember the flighty creature as a child, scurrying after her mother on the streets of Boston and that singular time in the forest when she had stuck her tongue out at him. More recently, before winter had covered New England with its characteristic blanket of snow, he remembered glancing outside his window—one day when Roger Chillingworth was in his room—and seeing Hester and her child walking through the cemetery.

"Mother, look at yonder Black Man," Pearl rattled away at her mother. "He has gotten hold of the minister. We must leave here or he will also catch us."

It was at that moment that Arthur began to regard old Roger Chillingworth as the enemy, his enemy. Was it not remarkable that it had taken a child—his own child, no less—to identify the source of his continual discomfort, that the child could see what its parent could not? He thought again of Pearl, no longer an infant but six, nearly seven, years old; her appearance still suggesting something not quite earthbound, but some free spirit capable of soaring into the air. She had grown so quickly that he was, in fact, surprised by her size. And what of Hester, whose face he was unable to see as the two of them walked through the garden? What had happened to her during these several years? Had she too changed as much as he? Perhaps mother and child had come to the cemetery in search of him, for he had long given up any hope of meeting them in the grotto in the forest.

In the evening—after his meal with Roger Chillingworth and the Widow Kellings—Arthur returned to his room, carefully closing the door behind him and wedging the back of an oak chair against the door so no one could enter his room unexpectedly. After pulling the curtains to his windows and lighting a candle, he removed his cassock and the undergarment which covered the upper portion of his body. The *A* was still lettered upon his breast, in no way altered since the previous time he had examined it. He looked at it for several minutes, contemplating the possibility that Roger Chillingworth was responsible for its appearance there.

How probable could that be? If Roger Chillingworth was responsible for its manifestation, then there had to be some reason. Furthermore, if the old man had conjured up its appearance, why had he chosen an *A*? Why not some other letter? Unless, of course, he knew about Arthur's relationship with Hester, but that was an impossibility. No one could read his mind. To be sure, the leech had determined that some terrible inner fear or guilt was eating away at Arthur's physical being, but how likely was it that he knew anything more than that? Arthur looked back at the *A* again, somewhat relieved for the first time in months.

Was it not more logical—as the old physician had further explained—that this physical disfigurement had been caused by his own excessive morbidity, that the mind under stress from unsolvable problems could lash back upon itself by torturing the body? That, too, was what the clever doctor had hinted to Arthur. It was either that or insanity: the mind could turn back upon itself, destroying itself, or take out its revenge upon the body. It was clearly a case of the latter.

It was impossible for Roger Chillingworth to know about his relationship with Hester Prynne. But why, then, did the leech persist in taunting him, making his days and nights a continual nightmare? Why was he constantly asking him to relate his dreams, his private thoughts, stories or incidents from his past? Why was he so insistent about these matters, unless—and here again Arthur could see no other explanation—he wanted to destroy Arthur's already precarious inner balance?

What, in fact, would happen if right now he would walk into Roger Chillingworth's room and tell him about his relationship with Hester Prynne? What would be the result? Pandemonium in the church, of course. But what else? Imprisonment, flogging, death? Yes, certainly all three, since as the masculine party, his punishment would be more severe than Hester's had been. And if not public execution, then public humiliation so severe that death would be the final outcome anyway. What would be worse at this stage, after all the years since Hester had suffered her own public humiliation?

But could he continue living under this sham, this religious charlatanism? Might not public exposure free him of the final burden of his heart? He examined his face in the mirror, surprised as he always was at the hollow expression that glanced back at him. He was reminded of the skull on Hannah Grey's tombstone, since his own flesh bore that same empty, sunken look. Might not a public confession free him of the unending debilitation and even, possibly, save him from everlasting Hell? Arthur sat on the edge of his bed examining the features of his face: the candle, glowing from the nightstand; the mirror, clenched in his hand at an angle that permitted light to fall upon his face; his head, reflected in the mirror as a skull, devoid of flesh and character. No, no, no, he screamed to himself—nothing could cleanse away a sin as ugly as his. Death was still the only alternative.

Candle—mirror—skull. The images swirled around in his troubled mind. His hands began to shake, his teeth to chatter. The ray of light from the candle—blinding when reflected from the mirror—the closeness of the room, the silence of the house. He tried to empty his mind of all superfluous thoughts, tried counting numbers so his mind would be freed of the burden of his decision. He could feel the warmth from the proximity of the candle and for a moment thought the ray of sharp, bright light had turned into a beam of hard metal that would pierce the pupils of his eyes.

"Confess!" the voice from the silence instructed him. "Confess your sins. It is your only hope. Climb the steps of the scaffold at twelve noon on the morrow and bare your chest for all to see. Confess, and purify your soul!"

Arthur fell back upon his bed and for the first time in many months entered into a deep, refreshing sleep.

Chapter Nine

MORNING brought release and a renewed sense of clarity for Arthur Dimmesdale. It was the first time in months, perhaps in several years, that his melancholia was arrested. The sun streamed in the windows of his room. The cemetery outside no longer reminded him of the inner gloom that had stained his personality for such an interminable period of time. As he climbed from his bed, Arthur felt a sudden intuition that his life of error and sham was about to be dramatically altered. Perhaps he would even be able to look back into people's faces and smile, rather than glance away and try to conceal his hidden turmoil. Perhaps it was not yet too late. His confession would change everything.

Quickly, he washed his face and hands with the water in the basin on his bureau, dressed himself with renewed concern, and hastened to the garderobe to complete his morning toilet. Glancing in the mirror on the wall, he detected an altered expression upon his face: not exactly happiness, but certainly not the hardened look that had marked his countenance for so long. When he glanced at his chest, after removing the garments from the upper portion of his torso, even the *A* seemed fainter, as if it were beginning to disappear. Unexpectedly, he was surprised at a fragment of music—a Monteverdi cantata that floated through his mind, some forgotten, but not completely lost piece of music from his student days at Oxford. For just a moment he stood there in the necessary house, permitting his memories to slip back to those untroubled days. Could that peaceful time be restored so easily, solely by his decision to climb the scaffold at noon and publicly confess his sins?

He tried not to think of the future and whatever alterations it would bring. He hummed sections of the cantata—not loud enough for anyone in the house to hear, but silently, at a level that engorged his aural sensitivities. Music flowed in and out of his head, not the pious hymns that he weekly heard issue forth from the clavichord in First Church, but an instrumental group with a choir, spreading through his mind. When he had completed his toilet and returned to his room, he wondered why he had never thought of these possibilities before: the renewing characteristic of music, its ability to transport the most depressed soul into new arenas of psychic freedom and release. What a fine world it would be once he had completed his public confession!

"You're looking fit this morning, Reverend Dimmesdale," Roger Chillingworth said to him, breaking the bubble in Arthur's mind and immediately reducing him to the peculiarities of the old man's sullen discourse.

The inner music stopped almost as quickly as it had begun. Arthur sat down at the Widow Kellings's table and tried to avoid a glance in Roger Chillingworth's direction.

"Have you had some good news?" the older man asked and thus continued before Arthur could reply: "Did the bell for the church finally arrive? As I returned to the house this morning, I thought I saw a new ship docked in the harbor."

"No, no, nothing like that," Arthur replied, his mood already regressing from the presence of the leech.

"It is this sunny day," the Widow Kellings interjected, after bringing her lodgers their morning soft-boiled eggs. "After all these weeks of rain, a little sunshine ought to brighten our lives." And—as she did most mornings once she had served their meal—she retired from the room, believing that the two gentlemen had more lofty conversation to engage in than her own limited gossip.

Arthur trembled as he broke the shell of his egg and scooped out a spoonful of the soft, viscous center. He started to move his hand to his heart but checked himself in time and grasped hold of the edge of the table for support.

"You look as if you have recovered from a long illness, brother," the older man stated. "You have regained some of your natural color. Methinks these warmer days will be a boon to you, now that we can continue our daily walks."

"I do not intend to walk with you any longer," Arthur replied, again avoiding a glance in Roger Chillingworth's direction. And then, surprised at himself, he added, "I no longer need your assistance. I have learned to help myself."

"You are well, then, Reverend Dimmesdale? You are cured of your malady?" The glance that came from the older man chilled Arthur Dimmesdale as if he had been splashed with a glass of cold water. He momentarily stopped eating his egg and swallowed a mouthful of tea.

"I did not say that I am cured—in the sense that you doctors of physic perceive of it."

"Then tell me, good sir, what happy occasion has befallen you and brought about this sudden transformation? Surely not the change in the weather our good landlady has suggested?"

"I am not at liberty to disclose—" Arthur began but abruptly stopped in midsentence. "Nothing has happened, Roger Chillingworth. I am the same as always, though perhaps as Mother Kellings says, I have of late been sorely affected by the continued spring rain."

Quickly—yet without appearing to act too rudely—Arthur finished his morning repast so he could return to his room.

"You even eat your breakfast with renewed vigor," the older man commented, seemingly aware of Arthur's every move and alteration. "As I have tried to tell you these many months, there is nothing better than a hearty breakfast to help us shoulder the most arduous days of our life. And this will certainly be a difficult day for you, my friend." The physician glanced back at his plate, as if it were now his turn to avoid a glance at Arthur.

Arthur moved his hand to his heart, thinking he could control the rapid beating he was certain Roger Chillingworth could hear from the opposite side of the table. In a trembling voice he asked, "What mean you by your statement?"

The older man remained silent for a moment, signaling with his hand that he would answer Arthur's question once he had swallowed the food in his mouth. For a minute, Arthur felt that Roger Chillingworth could read his mind and already knew of his intention to confess.

"Have you not heard?" the physician replied after a brief delay. "Governor Winthrop is worse and will probably not survive the day. I have spent these many hours with him during the night and only returned this morning for additional medicine to ease his journey to the other world."

Arthur felt that his skin had turned a pale white, a lighter color even than his normal peakedness. Death was making an appearance in his life once again and he was unable to do anything about it. Then Roger Chillingworth spoke before he was able to formulate any reply. "Reverend Wilson asks that you relieve him at noon, so that he may make the necessary arrangements for the funeral. Forgive me for not informing you earlier. I would have told you directly, but I hated to destroy your newfound state of serenity. We can, of course, never control these moments of death. They creep up upon us when we least suspect them. Were you not the one who said just last week that Governor Winthrop had never looked so healthy? I wonder if he has prepared himself for this inevitable shock."

"That is for him and his Maker," Arthur replied, rising from the table and walking toward the door.

"One moment, Reverend Dimmesdale," the older man called back at him. "Since duty takes us both to Governor Winthrop's side, shall we not walk together and enjoy the only pleasures of this fateful day?"

Back in his room, with the chair again wedged against the door, Arthur tried to pick up the pieces of his life, doubtful that he had the strength to endure the approaching events of the day. In a matter of minutes, his bitter freedom had been ripped away from him by this monster of inhumanity. There was some disturbingly uncanny aspect of Roger Chillingworth that Arthur had never been able to comprehend, to articulate—some perverse ability rooted deep within the older man's personality that gave to him the powers of a clairvoyant, a talent to read other people's minds and anticipate their moves even before they were certain of their own actions. Would he never be freed of this terrible demon who wrestled with his life? Would he be forced to live with this diabolical creature for all the remaining days of his earthly existence?

Arthur sat down on the edge of his bed, the melancholia of all the previous years more acute than at any time he could remember. His head ached, felt as if it might even explode from internal pressure. His body was again weakened by ague, and the disfigurement on his chest felt as if it might scorch his flesh. He pulled off his cassock and upper undergarment and reached for the mirror he had hidden away inside the hollowed-out book, but it was no longer there. The book was empty; someone had removed the profane object. He glanced down below his chin, trying to focus on the design of his flesh, only to be horrified by the discovery that it was darker, more inflamed than at any time since its original appearance.

What could he do? What was the next move? What would be achieved by a confession at this late stage except for an even more sudden encounter with death? He lifted his eyes to one of the windows in the room and glanced outside at the cemetery. He thought of Governor Winthrop's approaching demise. Everywhere he looked, everything he experienced brought him one step closer. And then there was Roger Chillingworth—Cerberus—pushing him nearer, then holding him back, but always controlling his entry to the portals of Hell. Would there never be any escape?

Moments later, after he had managed to collect his thoughts, there was a tap on the door of his chamber. "Just one minute," Arthur replied, quickly pulling his clothing over the exposed regions of his upper torso.

The tap continued. "Just a minute!" Arthur yelled back, a hysterical tone of his voice, he knew, again revealing his state of inner frenzy. Then he opened the door and faced the older man.

"Shall we depart for the governor's mansion?" Roger Chillingworth asked, immediately sizing him up with a contemptuous look.

"I am ready," Arthur replied, pulling the door closed behind him as if that were some symbolic indication that the older man should not enter his room uninvited.

They left the gloom of the widow's house for the bright sunshine outside, though neither commented on the beauty of the early day in May. They strode along silently, each man lost in his own private thoughts. The streets were empty except for occasional horse-drawn carts and passersby out for a late-morning errand. Arthur was conscious of the unevenness of the older man's gait, as if he had become more stooped in recent months. Walking down the street together, both dressed in their dark worsted garments, they made a gloomy pair, and Arthur suspected that they would not be interrupted from their course. Finally, the older man spoke:

"You know, good Reverend, I hesitate to mention this, but given the recent state of your malady and my own inability to assist you, I feel I must offer a suggestion I have frequently discussed with the good Reverend Wilson. There comes a time in every man's life when the best cure for a troubled heart is to take a wife." He paused for a moment, perhaps anticipating Arthur's response. "Have you not considered the possibility?"

"I am no longer young," the minister replied, looking straight ahead of him and avoiding the other's face.

"Nonsense! You are in the prime of your life—the ideal age," Roger Chillingworth retorted.

"My health would not permit it," Arthur shot back.

"That is the very reason I have suggested this matter, my young friend. Until you have enjoyed the advantages of married life, you will not know the benefits one may derive from such an arrangement. Certainly there are many fair maidens in your parish who would consider the opportunity an advantageous match."

Arthur cringed at the idea, his body trembling more out of emptiness than of fear. He straightened his shoulders as if that move would give him the necessary endurance to continue his dialogue with the learned physician.

"I know whereof I speak," Roger Chillingworth continued, "And would not make this suggestion lightly without some previous consultation with the elders of your church."

"You have known the comforts of wedded life?" Arthur asked him, surprised at the older man's revelation. Momentarily, he glanced away from the cobblestones on which his eyes had remained transfixed.

"It is never good for anyone to speak of subjects of which he remains unfamiliar, especially a doctor of physic. Let me tell you the story of my own married happiness as we walk toward the governor's estate, and perhaps it will aid you in your determination to see more clearly about this matter."

Arthur made no response. It was impossible for him to conceive of Roger Chillingworth in such a state—unless it had been many years ago, when the man was in his youth, and even then the idea was incongruous with the demon he now knew.

"I, too, was a melancholy youth—studious and above all concerned with matters of the mind. My parents were comfortable, able to indulge my intellectual interests and aid me in attaining my goals of the general requirements for the doctor of physic. Once attained, I pursued this profession year after year, unmindful of any other manner of life but the bachelor's way, and would have continued thusly were it not for an event that altered my life— transformed it, one might say—in the autumn of my patterned ways.

"You think you are too old to take a wife? I thought so too, but I was much older than you—much more given to life alone, the way I had always lived it and assumed I always would—comfortable, free of concern for others, except for my parents, of course, above all, predictable. Then an event happened that altered my life forever and is responsible, in truth, for my presence here today."

Arthur turned and looked at his companion, caught off guard by the latter comment.

"Aha! I can see I have taken you by surprise. You are amazed, of course, to learn that I, too, have given in to the emotions of the heart. I have not always been the way you see me now. It happened ten, maybe eleven years ago, when I was at the height of my profession, even looking forward to some kind of easier days in my declining years, some mellow period for reflection upon a life that had been satisfactory and comfortable in every way.

"One morning the civil authorities brought me a young woman who had tried to drown herself the previous night by jumping into the river. She was in a state of delirium, or so they told me, from the attempted suicide which had alerted the officials in the first place. It was my duty to try to bring her back to some state of normality so she could be brought to trial for her crime. No one knew her identity, having never seen her before, but as I was soon to discover, this was no simple case of shock or suppression. She had forgotten her past. She did not know her own name, where she had lived, or how she had gotten to London.

"She was an attractive young woman—somewhere in her late teens, I suspected—though it was clear that her body suffered from the lack of proper nourishment. When I examined her carefully, I suspected that a severe state of hysteria was clearly responsible for her forgetfulness, the unknown agitation of some recent event in her life—so horrible that she was forced to expunge it from her memory. What was particularly interesting, and the only clue I had, was a small silver object that she held tightly in her right hand. When she was fished from the river, the police had attempted to remove it from her fist, but she had clenched it even tighter and threatened to bite one of the men who tried to unarm her. To this day I can only be thankful that her fate was not that of so many attempted suicides—the insane asylum. Instead, she was brought to me for further examination.

"This beautiful, young woman would respond to my questions, but her answers little helped me understand the riddle of her identity. She simply did not know who she was. Her clothing—that of modest folk and well attended—revealed nothing else. There was only the object held tightly in her hand and, indeed, it took some days before she trusted me and permitted me to determine what it was. My housekeeper watched over her during the hours when I was absent in my surgery; I administered what care I could in the evenings, and after a few days she began to respond to our concerted effort to bring her back to the present world.

"A week or so after her arrival, she permitted me to see the ob-

ject in her hand—not touch it, I assure you—but allowed me to look
at it from a distance. To my surprise, the mysterious object was a
small silver cross, of no particular value—except to a believer, of
course. That gave us another clue—possibly this young girl was
some religious novitiate expelled or run away from a convent,
though that in itself presented a remarkable problem because she
had the darker features of a Jewess, especially the revealing nose.
With the aid of the authorities, I circulated a description of the
young woman's physical attributes—though not the fact that I believed she was Jewish—and then we waited to see if any news of
her identity was forthcoming.''

Roger Chillingworth paused for a moment as they turned a corner and started down another lane. Then he continued his story:

''There was no news about her identity, but there was other progress as the days turned into weeks, and finally months. This
young woman—her physical health now restored by proper
nourishment—began to remember things from her past, at first
images of places where she had been, but not yet proper names.
She cried out in the night, apparently from nightmares of the past.
Yet, she seemed to be responding to our care—perhaps because we
tried to instill in her a feeling of warmth and comfort and convince
her that no further harm would come to her now that she was under
our care. By 'our care,' I mean my housekeeper and myself, if you
understand what I mean?

''There were days when she seemed completely normal, gay and
full of life, except that she still could not remember her name or her
origins. She no longer insisted on having the silver cross on her
person; she worked around the house, assisting my housekeeper. I
even heard laughter coming from the kitchen, a rare sound from the
house of a settled bachelor. I had managed to convince the civil authorities to drop her case, pleading, I am afraid to say, a temporary
aberration, at least at the moment of her plunge into the river.

''To shorten my account, during the ensuing months I found my
own life remarkably transformed because of the growing attach-
ment I had made to her. I told myself that at such a time as she remembered her identity, I would ask for her hand in marriage,
though I already feared that she might not only remember her own
identity but a husband's also.''

''Did she never remember her name?'' Arthur asked, his curiosity having the better of him.

''You suspect, I feel, that she did not, since I am here alone. But
her memory did return. One morning when she came downstairs,

some half a year after her arrival at my place, she remembered everything. She simply awakened one morning with her full memory—an event that I can only conclude was brought about by her faith in the two of us who had watched over her. She knew her name; her date and place of birth; and remembered her arrival in Dover, where she had come to flee a local massacre of Jews on the Continent. You see, she was indeed, as I had suspected, Jewish, and she had had to flee from a small German town after the deaths of her parents, who were English, having moved to the Continent some years earlier. The crucifix was a ruse to fool the authorities who she thought were looking for her. She had fled back to England at the advice of some friends, and after several months when her money had run out and she could find no work or assistance from anyone, she attempted suicide by jumping into the Thames.''

"What was her name?" Arthur could not help asking, though for what reason he was unable to tell.

"Miriam Leveke," the older man replied, immediately adding, "and she shortly became my wedded wife."

"And you were not afraid to marry a Jewess?" Arthur asked him.

"It appeared of no importance then. It seems to have no significance now. Of course, others I did not tell."

"What happened to her? I hesitate to ask, since I fear she went down in the shipwreck that you survived."

"I do not know for certain. We lived happily for some months after our marriage, and then Miriam's health began to deteriorate again, though this time it was physical, not mental. In time my diagnosis revealed that she was suffering from consumption, as I had for some time suspected, and I as her physician recommended the best cure I knew: a voyage at sea, a new climate. In our haste to correct the illness of her body, she left England on a ship before I did. I was to follow shortly, once I had settled our affairs, for we agreed that perhaps the better plan was settlement in this new world where she would never need to fear a massacre again, such as the one that had taken her parents away."

"I understand now," Arthur replied, "how you came to this world alone and the greater loss you suffer from her memory. Perhaps some further inquiry will reveal that she survived her voyage, since certainly your own ship and hers would not both have gone down in the deep."

They had arrived at the governor's mansion and for a moment stood silently in front of the impressive structure.

"She has survived, of that I am certain," Roger Chillingworth replied.

"She is alive, and you have yet to go to her?" Arthur asked, perplexed by the older man's statement.

"Yes, my friend. She survived the voyage, but she is again another person—her recent identity lost forever to the past. But we must hurry, for I see Reverend Wilson waving to us that we are sorely needed."

Chapter Ten

Midnight came and passed. Boston was enveloped in a layer of
thick fog, the community asleep except for the occupants of Governor Winthrop's household: Arthur Dimmesdale, the most Reverend John Wilson, Roger Chillingworth, the governor's family, and
lesser functionaries. The silence in the governor's bedroom was so
acute that there was only the occasional forced breathing of the
great man about to make his final pilgrimage to the unknown. Arthur Dimmesdale and Roger Chillingworth had been sitting at his
side for more than twelve hours, except for those moments when
they temporarily crept away to revive themselves. The Reverend
Wilson, nearly in his dotage, had managed to sleep much of the
time since his return early in the evening. The room was so still
(the windows closed, the velvet curtains pulled to keep out evil
spirits) that even the dozen candles on top of the ornate deal dresser
and tabletops burned without a flicker. The room reminded Arthur
of a mausoleum.

He glanced around the chamber, squinted through his glasses
so he could focus on the various personages of the governor's
room: his fourth wife, soon to be his widow, her eyes reddened
with anguish and worry; Roger Chillingworth, hunched over in
his chair, the dark clothing and the angle of his body giving the
impression of some maligned creature—his eyes, Arthur knew,
closed but still capable of taking in every movement within the
room. John Wilson remained asleep as was one of the nurses
who had recently brought a pitcher of fresh water. Arthur settled himself more comfortably in his chair and then dozed off
for a moment himself.

* * *

He was awakened by the smell of sulphur and a chill upon his back—so cold, so sharp that he assumed that the governor had breathed his last breath. Without thinking, Arthur folded his arms in front of him and then watched in horror as the Devil arose from a gaping hole in the floor and stood over the governor's horizontal body. The Black Man hovered a moment above the governor's form and turned toward the other figures in the room as if he were considering the remaining possibilities for conversion. Arthur watched spellbound, detecting the expression on the face—the reddish skin, stretched tightly as if over a skull too large to fit the size of his body; the eyes aflame with fiery pupils, surrounded by a halo of whiteness that looked like a ring worn on one's finger or a piece of costume jewelry; the nostrils and mouth distended and gaping.

Arthur glanced down at the demon's feet, feeling the flames that were rising from the hole in the floor. Suddenly he was aware that the heat in the room was so intense that his shoes would soon begin smoldering. He lifted his feet from the floor, though he was unable to move the rest of his body or glance in any other direction. Then, through the flames and smoke, as if he were looking through some sort of veil obscuring another world, Arthur could see an endless chain of figures knotted together and burning in the flames of Hell: lesser devils linked together in one continuous rope, their bodies unclothed, their skin enveloped in the flames that lashed out to burn them. They held tightly to one another, using their arms and legs and their scrawny tails—their faces belying the acute discomfort of their pain. Arthur glanced at these subhuman creatures (dozens of them—no, hundreds) linked together, stretching endlessly down into the bottomless pit.

Arthur tried to close his eyes so he would not have to look at the abhorrent scene in front of him. He heard the cries of men, women, and children emanating from the hole—their pathetic howls of pain, more animal-like than human. He watched in horror as first one and then another was burned by the flames of Hell, pulling back their shriveled limbs in order to avoid the next tongue of fire. Yet always there was another flame to burn them, like the waves of the sea, lapping back, knocking them over—persistent, incessant, eternal. Arthur smelled the fire and brimstone, the hot putrid flesh. He listened to the painful cries, and then his eyes—unable to avoid the horrid scene—glanced at one of the faces of a lesser devil and discovered someone he knew.

It was Thomas Hooker, the famous Congregational clergyman, who had died two years previously and was assumed to be resting quietly in the firmament above. But, no, there he was, writhing in the flames and smoke the same as all the other lesser creatures around him. Arthur rubbed his eyes, but the spectacle before him would not go away. There were other faces he identified in the cluster of devils: the Widow Finney, that pious woman with whom Arthur had lived for the first few years of his life in Boston. What was she doing here? Her face revealed the same agony and terror as all the others, and Arthur tried to call out to her, but his voice would make no sound. There was only the silent plea on her visage, revealing the horror of her fate.

Then the faces came more quickly into focus: denizens of Boston he had known down through the years—good, simple people, often the pillars of his church; students he had known at Oxford, hearty, honest fellows, upright to the end. All were there before him; their faces all the same. Finally, in the parade of entangled devils, to his astonishment, Arthur saw his mother, her face devoid of any expression at all, as if she had suffered from some sudden paroxysm that had collapsed her mind. And Arthur realized for the first time since the pit had opened up before him that this was not a vision of Hell that was playing itself out in front of him, but worse: a vision of death, that certain hell toward which he moved inevitably closer each waking hour of his life.

He glanced up at Governor Winthrop's bed where the Devil was still standing, hovering over the shrouded figure, even the shiny black clothing on his back smoldering from the blazes of Hell.

A cry broke the silence of the room, a prolonged "*N-o-o-o-*" that went on for a full thirty seconds and then slowly faded out as Governor Winthrop gave up the ghost.

Arthur stood up from his chair, as the governor's last word was still fading away, blinked his eyes once or twice and identified the dark figure standing over Governor Winthrop as Roger Chillingworth. The room, which moments before had been as hot as an inferno, was as cold as the polar regions. The candles were flickering; there were muffled cries coming from the governor's wife and other members of his family. Someone had opened one of the velvet curtains to let in a little fresh air, though outside it was still as dark as the vision in Arthur Dimmesdale's mind.

* * *

Midnight had come and gone. Arthur climbed the steps of the
public scaffold, not fully cognizant of how he had managed to
arrive there. Reverend Wilson had told him to return to his
room and get some sleep, and though Arthur had agreed, he had
been afraid to walk through the empty streets, fearful of what
the night would reveal. Roger Chillingworth had said that he
would walk with the young minister, if he would wait until he
had made his final ministrations to the deceased, but Arthur—
even more afraid of the old physician than the black night—had
struck out on his own. It was not until he reached the safety of
his room that Arthur realized he had almost lost the perfect opportunity. Quickly he ran down the stairs, out the door, and
back into the darkened streets.

When he turned the corner at Prison Lane that brought him to
Market Square, he knew immediately what to expect. The scaffold
jutted out in front of him with such awfulness that Arthur wondered
if he had the strength to climb its manifold steps to the top.
Dwarfed at the bottom of the public structure, he placed his hand
on the rail and began his ascent. Each step reminded him of yet another of his innumerable sins: lust, adultery, and fornication;
pride, envy, and impenitence; fear and self-imposed isolation. He
counted the steps, the endless number of footfalls that controlled
each move of his lonely life. He counted the steps, knowing that
they would never end, yet ardently waiting for the ultimate one that
would release the heavy burden he had shouldered for so many
years. He counted the steps, waiting for the top where he would
publicly confess his transgressions.

Boston was asleep. It was a cool, almost cold, night in May;
the wind blew steadily from the sea. Hardly a light flickered in
any of the buildings that surrounded the square; no one was
about except for an alley cat that Arthur heard screeching somewhere in the distance. He raised his head and looked at the
heavens: the sky was sprinkled with specks of white, clustered
together in small groups as if they represented the spots of a
die; the moon had already sunk over the edge of the earth. No
one was about.

Arthur sighed, released the air in his lungs with such satisfaction
one would have thought he had been holding it there for years—
stagnant air he kept breathing in and out of his life. He closed his
eyes for a minute, then opened them and beheld the multitude in

the market: the citizens before whom Hester Prynne had stood seven lonely years ago.

Governor Bellingham and the lesser officials of the colony were sitting on the balcony of the meetinghouse, but they appeared to pay no attention to him. The market was flooded with hundreds of people: sellers of produce and other wares, farmers from the neighboring areas, families from the community. They went about their business, nary a one glancing in Arthur's direction atop the scaffold.

"I implore you to listen to me—I beg you to pay attention," Arthur pleaded, in a voice that he tried to raise above the general din issuing from the square. But it was not loud enough, and no one appeared to have heard his request.

"Governor Bellingham, I have sinned—" Arthur began, but the governor was busy talking to one of the elders and paid him no attention.

"I stand here before you a sinner—" Arthur yelled with all the pent-up fury of his voice, but he stopped midway in his confession when he realized that still no one was listening.

"Sin—" Arthur choked, holding on to one of the rails of the scaffold for support. "Sin—It is all We have." He held his head in his hands in defeat when he came to realize that no one cared about what he had to announce. He closed his eyes, and when he opened them a few moments later, the market was empty.

Then, to his horror, someone was approaching the scaffold. Arthur watched a light in the distance careen toward him, bouncing up and down, as if it were a lantern held by some goblin of the night. Arthur screamed, then held his breath, then screamed again—fanatically proclaiming his many sins, as if by this confession the spirit would pass him by, pay him no attention. As the light drew closer, he distinguished a dark figure holding a lamp, walking down Prison Lane in his direction. In a moment, he would no longer be alone—someone would be standing before him at the foot of the scaffold.

Arthur shouted out the list of his transgressions, confessed his sins, and then identified the shape with the lamp as old Reverend Wilson. Arthur shouted at his spiritual mentor, heckled him with his mockery, but the old man apparently heard no sounds from the scaffold. Rather, he kept walking at a determined pace, the lamp bouncing up and down with his jaunty movements, and finally turned down another lane and disappeared into the night.

* * *

Arthur screeched at the top of his voice, roared with such fury he thought his lungs would burst, expelled the ugly words of his confession with such volume that he feared the entire city would be awakened. He shrieked like a child, then like an animal—confessed his original sin and the seven years of hypocrisy. He babbled like an idiot, his body weakened by overexertion. In a final attempt to reveal his transgressions, he tore apart his cassock, and exposed his breast for all to see. But no one was about. No one was there to witness the fateful emblem. He glanced down his nose and tried to focus on his chest, but the light was dim and it was impossible to determine if the symbol was still there.

Then there were grotesque voices, whispers, the shrill laughter of unreal creatures, and Arthur knew that witches had surrounded him on the scaffold and were about to drag him off to Hell. He moved back as if to repel a blow, pulling his torn clothing over him. He felt a hand in his—the icy sting of death. He closed his eyes and passed out.

"Minister!" Pearl cried at him in her high-pitched voice—her hand in his, bringing him back to reality.

"Is it little Pearl?" he asked. "Is it truly Pearl and Hester Prynne?" He felt the child's warm hand enclosed in his, and though he was afraid to relinquish it, he needed to rub his eyes to determine if it were just an apparition. He lifted his glasses back enough to permit his fingers to massage his eyes, yet when he opened them again, Hester and the child—his child—were still at his side.

"Minister," the child continued, "will you stand with us in the daylight too?"

"Hush, child," her mother interjected. "The minister will meet with us in the daylight when the proper time arrives."

"Will that be soon? Tomorrow?" Pearl asked, again grasping his hand, now more tightly.

"Not tomorrow, but soon," Hester answered, as Arthur in the darkness of the night tried to restore the features of her face to his mind.

He trembled from the cold air—from the earlier exposure of his body—and then he asked her, "But what brings you here at this fateful hour of the night?"

"We have been to Governor Winthrop's to measure him for a shroud," Hester replied.

"Has the good governor passed away?" Arthur asked.

Before Hester could answer his question, Pearl—that flighty creature of the sky—tugged again at his hand and repeated her burning question: "When will you stand with us in the square, Minister? When will we meet again?"

Hester took the child's other hand as if to quiet her, and Arthur felt an electric charge jolt through his body, stood there transfixed, waiting for the crash of thunder that would certainly follow this flash of lightning.

"Hester, Hester, how have you been?" Arthur asked the scarlet woman in a faltering voice.

"The same as always," the woman replied. "Just as before. But what of you, Arthur? What has happened to you?"

"I am dying, Hester. Each day I feel my life being sucked out of me, each moment dragging me a little closer to—" But he could not complete his sentence, for Pearl broke away from Hester and with her free hand pointed below them, away from the scaffold.

Another figure was approaching the square. Though without a lantern, this one also cast forth illumination—eerie, reddish, suggesting some inner fire that served as its own source of luminescence. When the dark, misshapen form stopped at the edge of the market, Arthur knew it was Roger Chillingworth, come to haunt him even here. How ironic, he thought, that the craggy physician was the only one to witness his pantomime on the scaffold. And he knew, too, that old Roger Chillingworth would follow him to the corners of the earth.

Arthur held Pearl's hand more tightly, as if her fingers held all the support that would guide him through the ensuing years. Then the child pulled her hand away and quickly informed him, "You hurt my hand, Minister. You grasp too tightly."

Arthur was brought back to the present world. He glanced at Hester and then back at Roger Chillingworth who was silently watching the ballet on the scaffold, the fire from his eyes glowing even more brightly than before.

"I hate that man," Arthur told Hester, "he haunts me night and day."

And then, as though the leech had not heard his statement, he moved toward them.

"Did you follow me here?" Arthur asked the physician when he reached the side of the scaffold.

"Good Master Dimmesdale," the older man replied, "you should have waited for me at Governor Winthrop's."

"I know not of what you speak," Arthur replied, trembling in his steps.

"The night is chill and you are improperly dressed. If you are not careful, you will catch your death of cold. Come walk with me and I will guide you home." He made no reference to the presence of Hester and her child.

"I will follow where you lead me," Arthur replied in a voice suggesting that of a chastened child.

Without any good-byes, Arthur climbed down the steps of the scaffold and joined Roger Chillingworth who turned and began to walk in the direction of the Widow Kellings's house. Arthur followed obediently, though slowly, and it was necessary for the older man to look behind him from time to time to see if his ward was trailing him.

By the time they reached the house, Arthur Dimmesdale had fallen into a kind of stupor, wondering why he had let himself be dragged home like a naughty child. He wanted to lash out at the older man and assert his independence, but he lacked the energy for even a verbal attack on the old physician.

When they reached the door to Arthur's room, the leech inquired of him, "Do you need some assistance in getting ready for bed?"

Arthur snapped out of his lethargy. "I am fully capable of taking care of myself." Then he added, "I am not tired, and I do not intend to go to bed."

"But you must rest, good Reverend," the older man replied, a slight trace of a smile crossing his lips. "In the morning you have your sermon to preach—have you forgotten? You must conserve your energy."

"I am not tired," Arthur stated, striking the flintlock and lighting a candle.

"Let me give you something to assist you in your sleep. Surely you cannot stay awake all night and then preach in the morning."

"I want no more of your sleeping potions," Arthur answered. "They make me groggy for days on end and fill my head with strange, uncountable dreams."

"Then let me assist you in a far better way with no chemicals that will disturb your system."

"But I tell you," Arthur pleaded abortively, "I am not tired."

"All the more reason I should demonstrate for you an easier method for attaining necessary sleep." The older man inched his way into Arthur's chamber. Arthur knew there was nothing he could do to escape the physician's perverse intentions.

Arthur was about to sit down on the edge of his bed when he realized that he had lost his gloves. He considered mentioning this fact to his companion but remained silent; at least the air in his room counteracted some of the chill he had felt outside.

"We all have trouble attaining sleep at times," Roger Chillingworth informed him. "It seems to be part of the nature of our lives."

Arthur nodded and sat down on his bed, not paying much attention to the older man.

"You have certainly tried to put yourself to sleep by counting sheep, have you not?"

Arthur replied wearily that he had.

"There are similar and perhaps more successful ways of assuring one's sleep. But I will need one or two items to aid me in my demonstration. First, the candle," and he pointed to the flickering candle in its holder.

"I will not suffer any more of your painful tricks," Arthur proclaimed.

"Never fear. There is nothing you need worry about. I will only demonstrate what you may use in future times when sleep seems impossible and you cannot attain instant relaxation. Now, I will also need a mirror. Have you such?"

Arthur was afraid to look at the older man. After a minute he replied, "I do not keep such objects in my room."

"Well, never mind," Roger Chillingworth replied, "I will fetch one, since it is impossible to proceed without a mirror of some sort." He left the room, and Arthur trembled at the thought that the leech would shortly return with the pilfered mirror from his book. Was this another one of the old man's clever ploys? Arthur felt perspiration break out on his skin; the room was suddenly quite warm.

Then Roger Chillingworth returned. "Here," he said, holding out a small mirror Arthur had never seen before. "This is all we need: a candle and a mirror. Now the essential thing is to be as comfortable as possible, so you should take off your shoes and prop yourself up on your bed. After all, you are going to go to sleep."

Arthur did as he was instructed—anything so the older man

would leave his room more quickly. Outside it was still pitch dark, though he knew that soon the first rays of morning would shoot across the sky. Arthur removed his shoes and stockings, then leaned back on the pillows the older man had positioned against the headboard of his bed.

"There, that's good. Now, what I want you to do is tell me when you can see the flame from the candle reflected in the mirror—not your own face, but the flame, do you understand?"

Roger Chillingworth propped up the mirror on Arthur's nightstand with a small bottle, then walked across the room and lifted the candle from the dresser. After determining the proper position, he placed the candle on the chest at the foot of the bed, at an acute angle but on the same level as the mirror. "Can you see the flame in the mirror, yet?"

Arthur shook his head; the older man moved the candle.

"There," Arthur told him, his curiosity heightened by what was about to happen.

"Can you see it clearly now?" Roger Chillingworth asked him. "Is it centered in the mirror?"

"Yes, it fills the mirror. It is all that I can see."

"Good. Now without moving your hand or changing positions, remove your glasses."

"Remove my glasses?" Arthur questioned, "but you know I will not be able to see."

"You will see enough. The light is all you need to see for this exercise."

Arthur removed his glasses, surprised that the flame in the mirror shone just as brightly as before. There was, in fact, a kind of optical illusion. "Methinks that I am looking at the flame and not at the mirror."

"That is the intent," the older man replied.

Arthur listened to the leech's movements in the room and determined by the sound that he had seated himself in the chair near the window.

"Now I want you to listen to my voice, and repeat after me when I tell you—but only when I tell you, do you understand? Above all, keep your eyes focused on the flame in the mirror."

"All right." Arthur gazed at the mirror, already a drowsiness coming to his eyelids.

"Now listen to my voice." Roger Chillingworth paused for a moment and then began: "I am tired. I want to go to sleep. I am tired. I want to go to sleep. My eyes are tired. I want to go to sleep. My eyes are heavy. I want to go to sleep. Can you hear me?''

"Yes."

"Do not close your eyes. Leave them open until I tell you to close them. Now listen again, this time repeating each sentence after me: I am tired.''

"I am tired.''

"I want to go to sleep.''

"I want to go to sleep.''

"My eyes are tired.''

"My eyes are tired.''

The older man's voice droned on in a slow, monotonous rhythm. Arthur repeated each sentence in a whisper, duplicating the physician's more authoritative tone. He kept his eyes open, though the lids had become as heavy as metal. By the end of the sequence of phrases, it was all he could do to keep his eyes open and stare at the reflection in the mirror.

There was a lengthy pause and then the older man informed him, "Now close your eyes.'' Arthur did as he was instructed, still aware of Roger Chillingworth's voice, though at the same time feeling as though he were asleep.

"Can you hear me?''

"Yes," Arthur replied.

"You are now asleep," the voice informed him, immediately varying the earlier statement: "You are now asleep. When you wake up, you will feel refreshed, as if you have slept for eight hours. For eight hours,'' he repeated. "Do you understand?''

"I understand.''

"Good. You are now asleep. But you will follow my instructions. Listen carefully.''

Arthur listened to the commanding voice, knowing it would be impossible not to carry out its instructions.

"Lift your right arm in front of you, and raise it straight out so that it is parallel to the bed.''

Arthur did as he was told, surprised at the swiftness with which he followed the command.

"Now keep your arm where it is. It is light as air, and it will not bother you. Keep your arm in that position, until I tell you to move it.'' There was a pause. Then the voice continued. "Now listen carefully. You are in a deep slumber, but you can hear my voice. You are in a deep sleep, but you will follow my instructions. You are in a deep sleep, but you can open your eyes and you will not awaken. Do you understand?''

"I understand," Arthur replied.

"Open your eyes."

Arthur did as he was instructed, surprised to see his arm sticking out rigidly in front of him, surprised at the light in the room.

"You do not need your glasses. You can see without them. Now keep your arm in front of you. You are in a deep slumber, but you will follow my instructions. You are asleep, but you will answer my questions. Do you understand?''

"I understand."

There was a pause and then the older man asked, "What is your name?''

"Arthur Dimmesdale."

"Where were you born?''

"At Lyme Regis."

"When? What is the date of your birth?''

"January 14, 1610."

"How old are you?''

"Thirty-eight years old."

There was another pause and then the physician continued: "What were you doing on the scaffold in the market this evening?''

"I had gone there to do something."

"What was that? Why had you gone to the scaffold earlier this evening?''

"To confess."

"To confess what?''

"My sins."

"Are they many?''

"Yes, they are many."

"And you had gone to the scaffold to confess these sins?''

"Yes."

"Why to the scaffold—why not some other place?''

"It is where public offenders must confess their sins."

"And you have publicly offended this community?''

"I have sinned, Father."

"What did you call me?''

"Father."

"Why did you call me that?''

"Are you not my spiritual confessor?''

"That is correct. I am your heavenly father. Now tell me in what manner and wherefore you have sinned."

"I have been false to those who have been true to me. I have had no confidence in myself. I have lived by deceit and hypocrisy and have been unfaithful to those who have most needed me."

"Who are these people?"

"My congregation, my parish. My friends."

"Is there anyone else?"

"I have been hypocritical with everyone I know. I have walked amongst them and told them falsehoods. I have preached one thing and practiced another. I have polluted the environment in which I live."

"Are there other transgressions of which you have been guilty?"

"Yes, Father."

"What are they?"

"I have defiled my own body with obscene thoughts and acts."

"Were other people involved in these acts and thoughts?"

"Yes."

"Who are they?"

"The Devil—among others. I have been guilty of following the Devil and his many accomplices."

"Are there people of this community who have participated with you in these acts?"

"Yes."

"Who are they?"

"Good Master Chillingworth and Reverend Dimmesdale, are you well?" It was another voice, breaking into the monotony of the questions and answers. Arthur was aware of a strange popping in his ears, as if someone were snapping his fingers. He felt his arm crumble to the bed, and then he was suddenly awake.

"I saw a light coming from your room and heard voices," the Widow Kellings said in a chatty tone, "and feared that Reverend Dimmesdale might be ill or in need of some nourishment after such a long vigil at Governor Winthrop's."

Arthur placed his glasses back upon his face and looked at the widow, her nightdress pulled around her aged body.

"Never fear, good woman," Roger Chillingworth answered, bitterly. "Reverend Dimmesdale suffered from some inability to go to sleep. I was assisting him, demonstrating a way to induce slumber when one is tired but unable to sleep." He turned to Arthur and asked, "How do you feel?"

Arthur was surprised at the feeling of renewed strength that had come over his body. He felt as if he had indeed been awakened from a long night's sleep. "I feel . . . I feel as if I have slept through the entire night."

"Do you remember anything from your sleep?"

"Only the candle flickering in the mirror."

The Widow Kellings excused herself, after informing her lodgers that she would prepare their morning repast. Roger Chillingworth followed her out of the room. Outside, in the chilly morning air, day was beginning to break.

Chapter Eleven

EARLIER than Arthur had expected—soon after he had finished eating a silent breakfast with Roger Chillingworth—the gravediggers began their work on Governor Winthrop's earthly resting place. Arthur was sitting in a chair next to one of the windows of his room with his eyes closed, thinking about the curious events of the past twenty-four hours, when he heard a noise outside. When he looked down below him at the slope, he saw three men, digging away at the hard earth, still partly frozen from the harsh winter. They worked steadily, conversing with one another at the same time, though he could not distinguish their voices because of the distance and the glass in the windows that separated them. Although they had come to the cemetery dressed in old jackets and floppy hats, these extraneous items of clothing were shortly discarded. Arthur watched the macabre *pas de trois* for a few moments before closing his eyes again and thinking about the sermon he would deliver later in the morning.

Though he had closed his eyes so that he could concentrate more deeply, he was surprised by his heightened state of physical awareness. His body was relaxed from whatever Roger Chillingworth had done to make him fall asleep, followed by the hearty breakfast. He felt refreshed, a far cry from the enervation of the recent exhausting weeks and months. Perhaps there was, after all, something to the old physician's advice about the need for sleep, the need for deep relaxation and concentration. He would try the experiment again—but not in the old man's presence. He would barricade the door with the aid of a chair, light a candle, and position himself in such a manner that he could observe the flame in the mirror.

But first he would have to locate the mirror. He opened his eyes and scanned the room, wondering if by forgetfulness he had placed the forbidden object in some other hiding place after the last time he had gazed into it. For a moment he observed the gravediggers, but then shifted his glance to the objects within his room: the dresser, the nightstand, the fireplace, his bed, the chest, the cupboard, the pine shelf filled with musty, leather tomes. He arose from his chair and walked over to the dresser and began a search through the drawers among his clothes and the other objects he had stored there for the past several years: letters saved to be discarded at a future date, miscellaneous documents and drafts of his sermons, and here and there a religious pamphlet published long ago. But the mirror was nowhere in these drawers, as he had previously concluded.

He examined the clothing in his wardrobe in case by some oversight he had placed the mirror in a pocket of one of his garments and forgotten it. Then he glanced at the bed, thinking that it might be there; he lifted up the straw-ticked mattress and looked underneath. Someone had clearly removed it from his possession. Finally, he walked to the shelf of books and examined each one individually, but it was nowhere amongst them. Then, before he returned to his chair, something told him to look once again inside the book in which he had originally hidden the profane object, and there to his surprise he found the mirror, restored to its hollowed-out space.

The discovery perplexed him even more. Was his mind playing tricks upon him? Had the mirror been there all along, or had someone removed it and then—for whatever reasons—restored it to its original place of confinement? He did not know. He could not tell. Both possibilities disturbed him, since, in the case of the former, it meant that he was going mad—that he had reached the state in his confusion where he could no longer distinguish between what was and what was not. Yet if the mirror had been pilfered and then replaced, that was equally disturbing, since it meant that someone else was playing perverse experiments upon his already ragged mind, forcing him ever so carefully to the dark edge of existence. That person, he knew, could only be Roger Chillingworth, who surely had prowled around his room more than once during his absence.

But for what reasons? Of what interest could a pitiful soul like his own be to the old physician? The questions were too perplexing; they appeared to have no answers. He glanced at his clock and knew it was time to go to the church.

The sermon that Arthur preached was delivered with such fire and conviction that many of his followers were persuaded that their young minister's health had made a turn for the better. For his subject he had chosen the need for confession—the purpose it serves in each man's troubled life. Eloquently, he spoke of the need for each human being to have a confidant, someone to whom he can disclose his innermost weaknesses and misdoings, of the need for purging the mind of those daily fears and misgivings that when held inside gnaw away at one's conscience and debilitate his soul. In example after example, he related the desire for human compatibility as the true source of confession: for husbands and wives, gaining a mutual respect for each other by discussing their shortcomings; for parents and children, speaking freely to each other; for neighbors and friends, united by the open exchange of ideas. In short, he spoke of the necessity for a growing harmony among all men based upon openness and respect.

When he was ready to leave the church and return to his rooms—after declining a polite offer to share the Sunday meal with one of the families of his parish—he was stopped by the sexton, who appeared to be embarrassed at the need for troubling the minister with an insignificant matter. The dotty old church official was holding one of Arthur's gloves.

"Good Reverend Dimmesdale," the sexton began, "we have found one of your gloves."

Arthur stood in the narthex of the church, the whiteness of his flesh suddenly transformed by the flush of blood to his face.

"Thank you," Arthur replied, holding out his hand and taking the familiar object from the older man. Quickly, he folded it into an inconspicuous shape and held it in the palm of his hand.

"It was found on the public scaffold early this morning. We can only attribute its appearance there to the work of witches or Satan in an evil jest to make a mockery of our sacred ways. But a man of your esteem need never fear a struggle with the Devil, gloved or ungloved."

"Thank you, good friend," Arthur repeated, trying to leave the church as quickly as possible. "I had not noticed that it was misplaced."

"You must make a search to see if the other glove is also missing," the Sexton continued. "If that be so, then we must certainly send out a warning to others to be on guard against these evil happenings. Did you not see the portents in the sky last night, the strange configuration of the heavens?"

Arthur replied that he had not.

"We are yet of one opinion. Some of us conclude that they forbode renewed struggles with the savages of the colony. Others suggest a more peaceful existence for our sacred covenant— perhaps even a new era of enlightenment brought forth by Governor Winthrop's assured rest in the heavens. Whatever the case, be careful with your possessions. Lock them up, so that none of Satan's emissaries may fly away with them."

Arthur thanked the Sexton and made a hasty exit from the narthex.

In his room, later in the afternoon—after he had eaten still another meal with Roger Chillingworth and the Widow Kellings— Arthur attempted to reconstruct the events of the last few days: the old physician's confession of his former married state, Governor Winthrop's death, his own abortive confession on the scaffold, the encounter with Hester and Pearl, the induced period of slumber by staring at the flame in the mirror, the sexton's recovery of his glove. What did they all mean, these many unexpected events?

He stood near the dresser in his room and looked at the glove the sexton had returned to him, still folded over. It resembled a wad of discarded leather from some workman's bench, a scrap fallen to the floor. Carefully then, he unfolded it and placed it on his left hand, trembling slightly as he thought of the nearness of his public exposure. Fortunately, it was only one glove that had been discovered on the scaffold, dismissed by the sexton as one of Satan's tricks to discredit him. But what did that mean? Where was the other glove, since both were missing when he had returned home in the middle of the night? If its mate were subsequently discovered on the scaffold, would this still be regarded as witchcraft—or would it then be suspected that Arthur himself had stood upon the public structure during the night? What could he do? He sighed as he peeled the glove from his hand, knowing full well that he could not return to the platform to search for the missing mate. Rather, he would have to wait and see what next transpired, all because of his carelessness at dropping his gloves.

He placed the gauntlet back on the dresser and continued to regard it for another moment, realizing that in its singular state—without its match as it were—it would suggest to anyone who entered his room that its mate had been lost. Probably it should not remain in such a conspicuous place. Was it even possible, for whatever reason, that Roger Chillingworth had picked up the other glove and concealed it among his own possessions? No, the idea was too foolish. Certainly there could be no reason for that. But still, he should hide the existing glove so that no questions would be asked. He stood there a moment, looking around his room, wondering where to hide the object. It was the old problem of concealment, but finally he concluded it was best simply to place the singular glove in the drawer that contained other articles of clothing: undergarments, stockings, handkerchiefs, an older pair of gloves. If he rumpled the contents of the drawer, separated the other pair of gloves from each other, perhaps this one would never be identified as lacking a mate.

After completing this little act of deception, he sat down on the chair near the window and again reflected on the rapid turn of events of the past two days. He thought of Hester and Pearl with a sense of yearning, surprised at the stillness of his heart. Whatever Roger Chillingworth had done to him to induce a state of sleep—whether from an evil or a humane intent—he felt more relaxed, more peaceful than he had in months, and he wondered at this unexpected calm that had so rapidly overtaken him. What did it mean? What did it imply?

Suddenly, he thought of the *A* on his breast and wondered if it were still there. He rose from his chair—for a moment glancing outside at the pile of dirt at the side of the hole that had been dug for Governor Winthrop's grave—and walked over to the door and secured it with the chair. On his way back across the room he picked up the hollowed-out tome that contained the hidden object, only to discover that the mirror was missing once again.

His inner calm disappeared. The book fell from his hands and hit the floor, as Arthur's own life was catapulted back into the frenzy of the past seven years. Death was still stalking him. The open grave in the cemetery should have warned him. Mirror and glove. What was going on? Who was playing these tricks on him? He tried to collect his thoughts. He left his room for the garderobe where he could examine his breast in the mirror the widow had mounted near the tub, but even before he closed the door behind him, he noticed that the mirror in the bathing closet was also missing. Someone had removed it from the wall. He pulled the door closed and remained in the room for a minute so that no one would be suspicious of his move-ments.

When he considered that a safe time had elapsed, he returned to his own room, aware of voices coming from Roger Chillingworth's chamber. The older man was apparently entertaining some guest or, more likely, assisting some patient. Again, Arthur secured the door to his room as carefully as the chair permitted, then quickly removed the clothing from the upper portion of his body and tried to look down at his chest and determine if the *A* were still there. To his wonder, it seemed to have disappeared!

There was the usual problem: what object could he gaze into that would reflect the image on his breast? Still partly undressed, he walked over to one of the windows of his room—fearful that someone outside might observe him. To his amazement, he saw that the glove he had hidden away in the dresser only minutes earlier was now lying on the outer window frame, firmly held in position by a small stone.

Surely this could not be! He needed to take hold of himself. The window, the rock and the glove, the cemetery, and his room reeled around him. Events were closing in upon him so quickly that he wondered if, in fact, the Devil were not stalking him, forcing him to sign a pact so that he could be released from these horrible confusions. He drew back from the window and quickly pulled on his clothing. Then, standing back at the casement again he looked at the rock and the glove, clearly placed there by someone who was trying to drive him mad. He rubbed his eyes, but this was no optical illusion: the glove did not disappear. Then he turned the latch on the window and tried to force it up, but it would not budge. He strained with all his weakened resources, but the window was clearly stuck and would not open. Apparently, it had been nailed shut so that no one could break into the room.

What was he to do now? There were tears in his eyes as the frustration built up within his confused mind. He was about to turn and run outside and snatch the glove off the window ledge, but something told him to remain in his room, to keep his eyes focused on the object. If he went outside, it would be gone by the time he got there. In his anger, he pushed at the window again, strained every muscle of his body, yet the window did not move. The glove remained on the opposite side of the pane—inches away, yet out of his grasp. He considered breaking the glass but reflected on the difficulty of replacing the pane and the great inconvenience it would create for the Widow Kellings.

He remained at the casement, impotently wondering what he could do. Then he looked at the upper portion of the window, the top half, and thought that it might not be nailed shut; he might be able to pull it downward. Perhaps only the lower half was secured. He placed his hands on the upper portion, and after working it loose by continued jiggling, managed to move it slowly down. Minutes later, he pulled a chair close to the window, climbed up on it, and reached out and down for the rock and the glove.

To his equal dismay and relief, the glove was the right one—the mate to the one the sexton had handed him after the services in the church. His mind was not playing as many tricks upon him as he had feared. When he searched through the dresser, he located the mate where he had placed it. But how had the righthand glove appeared on the window ledge? No explanation was necessary for the glove the sexton had returned to him. Arthur knew he had lost both of them on the scaffold the night before. But what had caused the second glove to appear so mysteriously, carefully held down by the rock? Who was responsible for this latest act that had nearly pushed him over the edge of insanity?

He returned to the casement and closed the upper half of the window after throwing the rock through it as far as his toss could project. He sank down in the chair near the window, both gloves resting in his lap. What was happening? He closed his eyes and tried to think, but he could discover no explanation for the reappearance of the object on his windowsill. He opened his eyes and lifted the right glove from his lap. Perhaps someone had left a message inside it, a possible explanation for what had happened, but when he shook the glove and probed it carefully with his fingers he discovered that it was empty, just like its match.

About to fold them over and place them together in his dresser, he noticed that the thread that had been used when the gloves were originally sewn for him did not match, a curious fact that he had never noticed before. The left-hand glove was sewn with heavy, dark brown thread; that used for the right-hand one was considerably finer, though still a shade of brown—nor did it appear to be the kind of thread typically used for stitching leather. It was not nearly as strong. Examining them together, Arthur concluded that the thread in the right-hand glove was new—as if it had been recently replaced—though it was sewn with such perfection that there could be little doubt that it had been done by a master craftsman.

He began to turn the right-hand glove inside out to see if any other clues about its recent restitching would be revealed by such an examination. The leather, however, was hardened at several of the fingertips, and it was impossible to turn all the digits inside out. Close to the end of one of the fingers, however, he could identify additional stitching—not at a seam but where the tip of the finger would normally reside. After returning to his dresser and locating a penknife, he carefully removed the stitches from the seam in the finger where he had detected the additional stitching. With trembling fingers, he spread the opened piece of leather on his knee and read the message stitched thereon:

FOREST

A chill went up Arthur Dimmesdale's spine, creating a tingling sensation that restored the dormant passions of his body. After more than seven years, terrible years, Hester had sent him a message, the meaning of which was immediately clear: they were to meet together in the forest and renew their disrupted relationship. It was time for him to end his period of hibernation.

Everything began to make sense. It was Hester who had taken his gloves and then accidentally lost one of them on the scaffold. He looked at the word again, so carefully stitched in the finger of the glove, noticing for the first time a tiny, loose thread hanging down from the bottom of the *T*, the last letter of the word. Picking it up between his fingers and pulling on it, he watched the word unravel before his eyes, as did the forest in his mind.

Chapter Twelve

SEEMINGLY, the message stitched inside the glove was simple enough to decipher, but as Arthur was about to discover, it was not that easy to meet with Hester Prynne in the forest. Where in the forest? When? These secondary matters, Arthur learned, were far more difficult to determine than the meaning of the single-word communication. He could not simply leave his room that Sunday afternoon and return to their former meeting place of seven years before. How was Hester even to know that he had found the word stitched inside his glove, for certainly he might have tossed it with its mate into some drawer without examining it. Nor, Arthur realized, could he expect that Hester would be waiting at their meeting point the first time he returned to it. It would be a matter of chance, of several trips and additional messages possibly misinterpreted before they would be together.

During the ensuing days when he managed to resume his afternoon walks in the forest (the weather finally more conducive to that kind of exercise) Arthur began to wonder if Hester's message had meant their previous haunt, or perhaps somewhere else, deeper in the woods. The forest had changed during the seven long years since the day of Hester's public humiliation. It had been, in fact, nearly five years since Arthur had stopped going there expecting to meet Hester at their hidden shelter, and he was startled at the changes in the terrain. Milk Street, which lead to Winthrop's Marsh, was longer and wider—cutting deeper into the forest than it had those several years before. Then, too, woodsmen had wreaked their havoc on the trees, cutting randomly and without purpose, altering the texture of the forest that once had been regarded as a menace to the town.

The first day when Arthur attempted to locate their earlier meeting place, he was shocked to realize that the woods had so dramatically changed. The place of their retreat could not be found. Chopped down or overgrown, he did not know. But it was not where his memory told him it should be. For a while, the wild idea passed through his mind that someone had simply picked up their entire retreat and moved it somewhere else, so perplexing did this alteration strike him. Even the spring that fed the swamp seemed changed and not as he remembered it. In short, Arthur returned from the forest more confused than he had entered it, more unsure of where Hester had planned that they should meet.

A search several days later proved to be no more fruitful, and the same must be said of a third. The grotto had completely disappeared. The forest was simply too large for random encounters; they might walk around in circles for years. Nor, Arthur knew, could he afford to make his searches too obvious for fear that some third party would begin to wonder why the minister was resolutely exploring the area of Winthrop's Marsh. In an attempt to disperse any such suspicions, he varied his walks in the forest—often going far beyond the marsh in a more westerly direction. But even that diversion was risky, for almost always when he left the woods adjacent to the marsh, he encountered other people walking or children playing in the brush.

By the end of the third week of his searchings, he wondered if the message in the glove had been a figment of his imagination. Had it been Hester who had stitched the word there? Was his interpretation correct? Were they to meet again in the forest? When he examined the glove, which he had not yet taken to the cobbler to be resewn, he even doubted the existence of her message. The word was gone, of course, since he had unraveled it, but Arthur had begun to conclude that it had never been there in the first place. How was he to be certain that the message was not simply another one of Roger Chillingworth's perverse tricks to drive him mad? At the height of his confusion, he examined the glove carefully again and concluded that something had once been written there. But what the message had been, it was impossible to decipher.

As the days passed quickly by, as spring gave way to summer, and the return of new foliage in the wood covered the land with a bright, green lushness, Arthur realized that even more care would be necessary if he was to meet with Hester and Pearl, for someone else was also spending increasing time in the forest: Roger Chillingworth. The older man had once again begun his pillage of nature's bounty, searching in the dark recesses of the forest for plants and herbs of a medicinal value. Arthur would see him return from the woods, his gunnysack bursting with the labors of his search. More than once Arthur had feared that he would encounter the older man in the forest. Yet one matter had changed with the return of summer. It appeared that the old physician had temporarily decided to leave him alone. Their meetings were almost totally limited to sharing their meals with the Widow Kellings.

Toward the end of June, Arthur knew that he had interpreted the message in the glove correctly. He finally located the grotto, hidden by the dense overgrowth of seven years, the wall of weeds and shrubs so thick one would have concluded that it covered an entrance to some retreat filled with fantastic pirates' booty. Yet, it was still there—right where it should have been all along. Hester had made no attempt to make the entrance more visible; she had, in fact, been extremely careful that no plants or shrubs looked as if they had been trampled upon. But inside—inside the world which he had begun to think was limited only to his mind—there was no doubt about their once and future hiding place: the brush had been cleared, just enough so that he (or anyone else stumbling upon it) would deduce that this was some animal's lair. But it could not have been only the haven of some wild beast, since the location was the same as it had always been.

His heart beat rapidly as he realized that his searchings had not been in vain. Hester's message was clear. She was still waiting for him, as if no time had elapsed, as if those seven years had been completely eradicated. He sat on the ground—on the mat of soft pine needles and moss—and considered his course of action. The day before he had walked near the cottage on the coast where Hester and Pearl had lived for the past seven years, had stood off in the distance from their house with the hope of seeing them. It had been a foolish move, dangerous in its recklessness, but now he knew that an initial stage of contact had taken place. After relaxing for a few moments, he cleared a little more of the foliage in the hideaway so Hester would be able to determine that he had understood her message. They would still have to be careful, of course. It was impossible to leave any other kind of sign for her—one that indicated an exact time for their encounter, for instance—but he knew that it would be soon. His years of waiting were about to come to an end.

For several days it was impossible for Arthur to escape his obligations to his parish, but when he returned to the glade near the brook five days later after visiting the Apostle Eliot and his Indian converts, he knew that Hester had been there in the meantime and had detected the small changes he had made. The retreat was as it had been the previous time, when he had cleared away more of the foliage. Yet she had left a mark this time—without changing any of the inner appearance of the brush—that only he understood, for caught on one of the branches inside the grotto was a piece of brown thread. It had been made to appear that it had perhaps unraveled from the clothing of some hunter or trapper who had stalked through the bush. When he held it in his hands and examined it carefully, Arthur recognized it as the thread that had been used to stitch his glove—the one that Hester had removed before she restitched it with her message. It was still bent unevenly, in a zigzag manner, from the original stitching. He rolled it around one of his fingers and then placed it on one of the pockets of the lining of his cassock. Then he relaxed on the moss again, listening for whatever noises were mingled in the background din, his mind slipping back eight years to his initial encounter with Hester Prynne. The thoughts flowed quickly as he reclined upon the ground, propping himself up with one elbow, his heart beating with the passion of his initial encounter with Hester Prynne.

Whether or not it was the bird that had drawn him to her in the first place, he would never know. A sudden rush of emotion had filled him with fear on that summer day as he fled through the forest, quite lost in his attempt to locate the path for his return home. Earlier in the day, in the morning, he had visited one of his ailing parishioners who lived on a farm outside the town. The mission completed, the patient's wife had suggested that Arthur take a shortcut home through the wood, crossing near Winthrop's Marsh. Against his better judgment and largely so that he would not appear weak-spirited, he had followed the path of her instructions, afraid, as he had always been, of the wild bush. Inevitably, he had become lost, and in his panic had left the path and run blindly through the woods, tearing his cassock and nearly losing his glasses.

Hysterical from his fear of the great unknown, he had finally managed to gather his senses. He stopped running, stopped fighting the thickets and brambles and sat down on a fallen tree and tried to collect his wits. It was still the middle of the afternoon. He told himself that there could be no fear of darkness trapping him in the forest. Though it was difficult to tell the exact location of the sun because of the thick overgrowth that surrounded him, he knew that darkness was still several hours away. As he sat there panting, the bird began its rapid pipings in the distance, shattering the silence and informing him that all was well. It was not a squawk of warning. It was simply the usual chirruppings of a chickadee. There was nothing to fear.

His worries controlled—his heart no longer beating with rapid fury—he rose from the tree and tried to determine the direction of his return home. Then he walked slowly, stopping every few minutes to listen for sounds that might guide him on his way. He had not gone far when he heard the gurgling of the brook in the distance and knew that he was no longer lost. The spring off High Street that flowed into the marsh would lead him out of the woods and back to the town. About to advance through a clump of creepers near the brook, he heard the splashing of water and realized that he was not alone. Someone or some creature was bathing in the water, splashing noisily about without any care of discovery.

He crept more slowly toward the creek than he had moved before, in case the noise had been made by some creature that might attack him if suddenly threatened by his appearance through the brush. The maze of maple and hemlock trees made it difficult for him to perceive a window on the brook, but walking a short distance upstream toward the direction of the splashes, he soon came upon a wider expanse of water—a small pond, fifteen or twenty feet in diameter. As he stood there watching, a figure stood up in the shallow water—a woman with her back glistening in the sun's sharp rays. Arthur closed his eyes and muttered a silent prayer, as the earlier rapid beating returned and began to course through his heart once again. Though it was difficult to identify the bather in the pond—so reckless and untroubled in this state of natural purity—he shortly recognized the woman as one of his younger parishioners, Hester Prynne. Though he knew it was a sin for him to watch her at her ablutions in the brook, he stood there transfixed, holding his breath and watching the carefree creature in the limpid water, as if she were the sole possessor of this body of effervescence where nothing could ever intrude and destroy her harmony with the wood.

After assuring himself that he was protected by the bushes, he squatted down on the bank and watched the naked swimmer glide back and forth through the water. She appeared to be enjoying herself so fully that Arthur wondered if she were really alone, if she weren't swimming with some companion or invisible lover, but as far as he could determine there was no one else in the water and no one on the banks. Though the upper portion of her body arose from the water measurably whenever she changed directions, the lower regions remained obscured. Still, he was surprised, even shocked by her nakedness. There was nothing covering her body at all. She wore no garment at all, a marked contrast to his own practice of always keeping one article of clothing on his body when he bathed. This was not true of the figure in the pond; she was as naked as Eve in the Garden of Eden.

When she left the water and retreated toward her clothing scattered upon the opposite side of the brook, Arthur closed his eyes. He released the branches he had pulled back to observe Hester Prynne more carefully and then sat there breathless, wondering what might be his next move. If he stood up, if he changed his position, he would certainly be noticed by the woman, and probably she would surmise that he had been spying upon her. If he remained there squatting on the ground until she had finished dressing, he would have to return to the village alone and possibly run the risk of getting lost a second time. He could not tell how long he had been observing her, but the sun had changed its angle again and there probably were only two or three hours remaining before darkness.

He moved the branches back again so that he could glance across the brook and see if Hester Prynne had finished dressing. The pile of clothing was gone; and to his surprise, she was no longer standing where he had last observed her. She had disappeared! Quickly, then, he stood up and pushed the branches apart and advanced a step or two to the edge of the brook, hoping to catch a glimpse of her as she walked back along the edge of the creek, but she was nowhere to be seen. She had not only completely vanished, but she had disappeared without making any sound, her retreat through the woods as silent as her earlier glide through the water.

Arthur froze. Momentarily, he considered shouting in the direction she must surely have taken—yelling after her, but he stifled his voice, fearful that she would conclude that he had been watching her. For a moment in his befuddlement he was not even certain which direction was upstream, the course that would take him to his objective, the spring that fed the brook. He collected his thoughts, realizing that his first action should be to cross to the other side of the stream and locate the path Mistress Prynne had surely taken homeward.

He looked in both directions for some favorable site for fording the stream and hurriedly determined the best choice—just before the pond, where the water had been banked up. Noisily, then, walking through the brush, he reached the safest place to cross with only the threat of partial submersion in the water. Once there, he stopped in his tracks and again listened for sounds of Hester's hasty retreat, but the forest was silent except for the natural cadences produced by birds and insects. He stopped to remove his shoes and stockings; then grasping them in one hand (the other holding up the hems of his cassock) he began to wade through the water to the other side, slipping on stones, occasionally sinking a few inches into the silt of the creek bed. As he reached the other side and was about to scramble up the sharp embankment, he fell into the brook, drenching his clothing in water and mud, but fortunately not losing the objects in his hands.

In the moment of his mad scramble to grasp hold of the bank, retain his shoes and stockings, yet not completely cover himself with water and slime, he thought he heard someone laugh—giggle perhaps—but he was not certain because of the concentration needed to keep his balance and not totally immerse himself. A moment later, when he stood safely on the bank, his cassock stained with water and mud, he knew he had been right. The laughter was repeated, followed by Hester's questioning voice, "Arthur, Arthur Dimmesdale, what a sight you make." The young woman appeared before him, emerging from the trees, stifling still another laugh.

"Hester, Hester Prynne, is it you?" Arthur asked sheepishly, looking down at his soiled cassock. He stood in front of her, holding his shoes and stockings awkwardly in one hand.

"We will have to do something about your clothing before you return to the village," Hester suggested, still hiding the laughter that was in her soul. Suddenly, Arthur realized that she had also been observing him for some time—had watched, no doubt, his entire attempt to ford the stream.

"I tore my cassock in the woods," he informed her.

"And now it is covered with water and mud."

"Methinks I can go back this way without causing that much of a scandal. It is not the first time I have fallen into water." He was about to bend over and pull on his stockings and shoes.

"There is no need for that," Hester Prynne replied. "Just go in there and remove your cassock, and I will wash the mud away from it," she continued, pointing to an opening in the brush.

Arthur immediately blushed at her suggestion, astonished by her forthrightness, but she pushed him in the direction of the opening before he could respond. "Now do not be afraid. I will not watch you. You can throw the garment out to me and I will clean it in the brook. You will look like a fool returning with it covered as it is.''

When she nudged him a second time, he did as she suggested, surprised—once he had crawled through the opening in the brush—at the grotto he had entered. It was a tiny room, hidden away in the woods near the side of the brook, which someone had obviously fashioned as a kind of secret retreat. Though he could barely stand up, he stretched himself, first making certain that Hester would not be able to observe him; then he pulled off the mud-speckled cassock and tossed it to her through the hole in the wall of the foliage. Though he would have been embarrassed for anyone to see him, he was in fact fully covered by his undergarments.

"I will just be a minute," he heard Hester say, then listened to her retreat into the distance. Arthur huddled inside the grotto, wondering what he should do while he waited. Sit down? Replace his stockings and shoes? But they too were smattered with mud. In order to still the beating of his heart, he tried to occupy himself by removing the filth on his shoes, rubbing them against the branches and leaves that circumscribed his temporary hiding place.

A few minutes later he heard Hester's voice, "Do you want me to try to dry it off in the sun, or do you want to put it on the way it is?"

"I think I had better wear it as it is," he replied. "It will take too long to dry; it is already later than I had expected to be away."

The cassock was pushed back through the wall of shrubbery, damp but now clean of the offending slime. When he took hold of it, he realized that Hester had not let go. Then there was a flood of sudden brightness, even inside the thick foliage, as Hester Prynne crawled through the brush and stood before him, her long, dark tresses—which minutes earlier had been tied up on her head—cascading down over her bare shoulders.

Afterward—when it was still too early for the guilt, the suffering, and the pain to grasp hold of him—he marveled at the suddenness of the transformation. Not a word had been said beyond the howling repetition of each other's names. His clothing, except for the undergarment he had insisted on keeping on the upper portion of his body, was strewn about the grotto, beneath them and off to their sides. One shoe still had a stocking dangling from it; the cassock would need to be washed a second time, and he himself would need to bathe in the stream. How could this be? Arthur asked him-

self, dumbfounded not only by the sudden passion that she had un-
leashed within him, but his equal surprise that they were both
virgins.

"But you were married, Hester, these many years?" he blurted
out in his confusion, wondering from his limited notions of sexuality if something had been wrong.

"In name only. True, I have been married, but I have had no
husband. I have known no man," and she pulled him closer to her
as if she were protecting herself from dark, uncontrollable shadows
over which she had no sway. He looked up into her face, blurred
because he had removed his glasses, and then above her at the sparkle of diamonds that entered their haven from an occasional opening in the canopy of leaves.

A moment later Arthur replied, "But he sent you here to wait for
him, to make the necessary preparations for his arrival." He was
aware that he did not know the name of Hester's spouse and he was
afraid to ask. As long as her husband remained nameless, he had no
identity of his own and they were protected from his appearance in
the land.

"That is true, in part. Our agreement was such, but that was
never my intention. When I boarded that fateful ship, when I began
that wretched journey, I knew that we would never live under such
false pretenses again. I ran away from him. The fates have carried
him where they will. I am free. Though he should appear inside
this refuge this very minute, I will never acknowledge his existence. I owe him nothing."

Arthur trembled at the mere suggestion that Hester's husband
might appear before them. He looked around at the protective
bower of brush that cradled them, then reached for his glasses and
repositioned them on his nose. The effect of the lenses was as if he
had donned a differing morality. He was afraid to look at the
woman who had positioned herself at his side, afraid to glance at
her flesh. He reached for an article of clothing to cover himself.

"But he is your husband. Whether in name or action, the effect
is the same," Arthur continued. "We have committed adultery."

"That is not so. There can be no adultery without a third party.
Nothing has changed, because there never was anything in the first
place. I have had no husband. I have none now. I am a free spirit,
and we are free to do as we please."

"This will require some further meditation," Arthur mused
aloud to her, and then he paused. "But come, we must hurry. It is

getting late. We must return before darkness casts its final shadow before night.''

''I see no shadows in our future, Arthur, unless we cast them there ourselves.''

Quickly they washed in the brook, separately, and pulled on the clothing that would disguise them from the world around them. Then they returned to the village, separately as they had left it— enveloped in a mist of loneliness.

Eight years later, again sitting inside their secret hiding place— after an interval of nearly five years when he had concluded they would never meet again under such circumstances—Arthur felt the renewed excitement of their expected encounter swell inside his breast. He removed the rolled-up piece of thread from his cassock and unraveled it between his fingers, still filled with wonder at the ingenuity of Hester's message to bring them together. He listened for indications from the wood, for any sign that this was the time when they would meet again. Momentarily, he was disturbed, realizing that it might still be days, even weeks, before they could both arrange to return to the woods at the same time and meet alone after so many troubling years. How long would this waiting last?

His thoughts slipped back a second time to their initial encounter eight years earlier, to the aftermath of their original meeting. Even that soon there was the despair of emptiness, of returning to the village separately, the beginning of their days of mutual concealment. He recalled a later meeting when Hester confessed that she had planned the entire episode that first time, swimming naked in the brook in order to tempt him. ''I knew that you were watching me while I was bathing. I heard your flounderings in the wood.''

''And you did not try to help me find my way?'' he had asked her, astonished by her boldness.

''Yes, I helped you find your way,'' she coyly replied. ''Never did you look as foolish as the moment when I fished you from the creek.''

''You did not fish me out of the brook. I climbed out by myself, by my own volition.''

''In a manner of speaking, yes. I feared I would not be able to convince you to let me wash the mud from your clothing.''

It was one of the few overt references to sexuality during their brief relationship, one of the few times when she had managed to make him happy and remove the cloud of guilt that had quickly positioned itself over his head. As he recalled their dialogue, he twisted the piece of thread around another finger, wondering if it might be possible to return to those former days. He had lost the most important moment of his life. Why had he refused to let this woman—who knew so very much about living in spite of the troubles she had encountered—liberate him from his fears? Why had he sunk into such a miasma of hypocrisy, when all that had been demanded of him was a simple act of assertiveness?

Arthur sat there quietly in the grotto filled with despair, his body huddled up and shivering though it was a mild summer day. He wrapped his arms around his shoulders to keep warm. Deep inside himself he already knew that it was too late. He was incapable of any assertive act except for acquiescence. He unwound the piece of thread from his finger and let it drop to the ground. He was about to crawl through the shrubbery and return to the village when he heard a noise coming from the distance.

His body twitched again. Someone was fast approaching his hiding place—someone who he knew could not be Hester Prynne. The noise was too unruly. If Hester had returned to meet him, her arrival would be silent and secretive—no one would be aware of her movements. But this was something else—the flighty motion of some object of destruction, perhaps some creature of the wild, blindly charging through the wood. He tried to conceal himself carefully in the grotto, his curiosity at the same time tempting him to learn the identity of the advancing figure. With one hand, he made a small opening in the leaves that surrounded him and positioned his face so that he could observe the outside world.

The noises continued, human sounds he now recognized as vaguely familiar. Then a moment later, he saw the child tear through the woods in her hurry to reach the side of the brook. It was Pearl, his own ill-begotten child. How was it that he had forgotten that any encounter with Hester would also have to include their child? He shrank back into the retreat, again permitting the leaves to conceal his presence and his proximity to the wild child at play on the bank. Quickly, he glanced behind him, wondering if there were not some other exit from his retreat, some escape route that would permit him to avoid the awful reality of their presence.

Chapter Thirteen

"**D**o not worry about Pearl," Hester admonished, a few minutes later, as she broke through the wall of leaves. "She will play at the brook while we talk." The child had remained at the side of the water when Hester had walked toward the grotto where Arthur was trapped, as if by some intuitive sense she had known all along that this was the time the minister would be waiting for her.

There was an awkward moment as Hester settled herself comfortably on the ground close to him. Arthur was not sure about what he should say, was almost afraid to look at her, but then she broke the silence, "It has been so long, Arthur. How are you?"

"I have survived, as you have," Arthur replied, his hand moving to his breast. "We have survived." He looked around the bower, suddenly feeling quite out of place, as if he were talking to someone from some other life. Then he looked directly at Hester for the first time since she had entered their secret cavern, startled again at her beauty, so hidden from the mundane realm of Boston's important men and women. Her dark, penetrating eyes drank in the suffused light that surrounded them, mirroring the best in even this most forlorn of worlds where Arthur had begun to feel a prisoner.

"I worried the night after Governor Winthrop's demise—when we found you on the scaffold." Arthur was aware that her sentence was not in the singular. There was that telling reference to the third party, the child at the brook. "I have been so worried since that night. You have not found peace, Arthur?" He wasn't certain if her last sentence was a statement of fact or a question. There was another silence while he listened to the child in the distance, splashing in the water. He was almost afraid to answer Hester's question. What could be achieved by coming together again? He did not know if he had the energy to resume their relationship where it had been interrupted so long before.

"I have been afraid for you, Arthur, all these years, but until the night on the scaffold, I did not know what"—and she stopped talking in midsentence—"I did not know how troubled you have become."

"Hester, I am most miserable. I hardly know what I have been doing, yet I know that everything I have done has been wrong. I am afraid of life, but even more afraid of death, and being trapped between the two has been a most wretched existence. I do not know where to turn."

Hester reached out and took his hand in hers. "I have made errors, too, Arthur. I have made wrong decisions that only recently I have been able to understand."

"But you wear your mark in public, Hester, for all the world to see. Mine is borne in secret, always cutting deeper into my soul." He glanced at the needlepoint letter on her bosom, envious of the symbolic mark for the first time since the day she had graced it. The letter moved up and down, ever so rhythmically. How could this letter, so exquisitely embroidered, be considered a symbol of something so negative? For a moment he thought he might be entranced by the steady movement of her breast. "I have heard nothing about you these many years that has not been favorable. The people call you a sister of mercy. By the letter on your breast, you have been transformed into something most admirable. There is no stigma now when you walk in the village. While as for me, I cannot stand in any crowd without knowing that I have lived these thousand years a hypocrite in their very midst. You have become what I am assumed to be: a Visible Saint. Nothing is as it appears. Our roles have been reversed."

"You make more of our differences than I would have you assume. I daresay this image you use to describe yourself is yours alone. It is not supported by your popularity among your parishioners. They feel that you have attained the pinnacle of success for someone so young."

"My ministry has removed me from the very people I have professed to help. It has not only made me old beyond my years, but a stranger to my people and myself, an observer like old Roger Chillingworth. I stand off at a distance, an outsider, always looking but never becoming involved in anything but my own unending flight from myself. While you, Hester, by your good works have been transplanted to the very center of the community. I live alone not even knowing myself, always fearing that our act will be discovered. Yours is known and it has set you free to do as you will.''

''But the people love you also, Arthur, by your good works more than anyone else—even old Reverend Wilson.''

''All sham, Hester. It is all sham. I cannot live with myself. I cannot withstand this internal agony any longer. What good is this public support if a man cannot stand a moment alone without fears of destruction? How am I ever to escape this travail?'' She rubbed his hand gently, as if she were removing some fatal stain.

''The source of all your agony lives among us. As much as you, I have been guilty of making wrong decisions about our past and our future.''

''I know not what you mean. We did as we could, but all was based on fear. What else could there be to rule our lives?''

''Arthur, the root of your daily agony is not limited to this concealment, but the man, I fear, who shares your every waking hour and even your sleep—old Roger Chillingworth. It was he whom I called my husband before the ship brought me here.''

Arthur jerked his hand free from hers and moved to the back of the grotto as if he had been struck by some fatal pain, the expression on his face altered to that of a madman, wild with fury. ''No, Hester, tell me this cannot be true! You jest, yet I must surely have known all along. The parasite lives on its host often because the organism permits the relationship in the first place. Oh, Hester, if this is true, you have most grievously wronged me. I have been mortally wounded by this fiend, who has lived on my very wretchedness. You have wronged me most terribly.''

''Arthur, can you forgive me? It was my error alone, made in fear at the moment of my greatest weakness. You are not the only one who has lived a life of concealment. I cannot exchange the past for any other. I take responsibility for that miscalculation, but can you not remember the day of my public exposure on the scaffold, the frenzy of those hours, the madness that I too endured for fear of your exposure? It was at that very hour when Roger Chillingworth tricked me into keeping his identity a secret—when I was at my weakest, the afternoon I feared for Pearl's life. I knew not what to do.''

''I should have known even then, Hester. From the very moment I first set eyes upon him, something was not as it should have been. Oh, what a monster has dwelled in our midst!''

"Can you forgive me, Arthur? Can you forgive me now?" She inched a little in his direction, reaching out to take hold of his hands once again.

"You are forgiven. There was nothing else you could have done." Arthur moved back to the center of the bower where they had been sitting, suddenly knowing that by talking to Hester, even though she was his companion in crime, he would be cleansed of his stains. Perhaps she could help him dissolve the miseries of their past, the errors he had lived with for so many haunted years. He glanced again at the *A* on her bosom, aware of the potential freedom the emblem might still hold in store for him.

"Arthur, the most difficult moment of my life was not seven years ago when I stood on that platform with Pearl, as awful as that may have been, but last month when I discovered you standing there alone, the night of Governor Winthrop's ascent into the heavens." She grasped his hand more tightly, and Arthur felt a sense of renewed strength passing from her body into his. "It was not even discovering you alone confessing your sins, but Roger Chillingworth's power when he plucked you away from us as if we had not been standing there. Then I knew that mine was a greater miscalculation than yours."

"It has been a most wretched time, Hester. The fiend will not leave me alone; he spies on me every moment of my life." Arthur glanced around their bower, as if he expected to see old Roger Chillingworth in their midst. "But I am confused, Hester. I do not understand how this evil man can be your husband. He has told me himself of his previous life in the old country and described his lengthy captivity with the Indians and it seems not to relate to what I know of you. How could you ever have been the wife of this demon?"

"I was not his wife, as I told you long ago. He was my husband in name only. We shared a common name and that is all."

"Prynne?" Arthur asked her.

"No, not even that. I took that name when I arrived here, determined never to live with him again—just as he assumed a new surname when he discovered me with Pearl. I thought my name would make it more difficult for him to follow me, if ever he tried to do so. We both have different names than before. His name was Kursar, though that also had been altered years before from his family name. Roger was his given name. Roger Kursar. Mine was

Leveke, and the given name was Miriam. When I married him, I was called Miriam Kursar.''

''But how could you have married such a monster in the first place?'' Arthur asked her, the pitch of his voice elevated as if to wring the answer from his companion.

''It was not my choice, as you can surmise. I had no say in the matter at all. I did what a dutiful daughter was expected to do, even willingly you could say, since I loved my father and even today, were he alive, would have difficulty going against his request.''

''I could have assumed such an arrangement. But why would your father choose someone like Roger Chillingworth?'' Arthur asked, then added before she had the chance to reply, ''I cannot refer to him by any other name since that is what I have learned to call him.''

''I, too, now think of him as Roger Chillingworth. It is the only thing that has made his presence here tolerable.'' She paused for a moment before answering Arthur's question. ''We were a poor family, always living on the edge of starvation. My mother died when I was still a child; my father raised me as best he could. I doubt not his love and devotion to me, since nearly everything he did in life was to keep the two of us together, to help me as a child. But he did not possess the proper disposition to enter the numerous ventures he engaged upon. His inherent honesty became the major contribution to our continual poverty.

''There is no need for me to chronicle the string of activities upon which he embarked, always undertaken as the enterprise that would elevate us above our precarious existence. There were many, and Father was always going further into debt, while others—his ofttimes more unscrupulous associates—frequently became successful in ventures he had started and then left at inauspicious times. We survived from year to year somehow, and from the distance now of this past decade, I do not believe that things were ever as bad as he convinced himself they were. He simply desired something better, for me, at least.''

''Where does Roger Chillingworth enter into this?'' Arthur asked, feeling a chill overtake him even as he pronounced the old man's name.

''I am coming to that. It was while I was still an adolescent, about fourteen or fifteen. My father's latest venture a failure, he had taken a position in a tavern, a kind of music hall actually, where entertainers would come through to perform for a week or so and then move on to some other location—actors, singers, acrobats of one kind or another. It was my father's duty to make the proper arrangements for these itinerant entertainers. He was a kind of manager, you might say, though in the employment of the owner of the drinking establishment. Roger Chillingworth was one of the entertainers.''

"One of the entertainers?'' Arthur asked, aghast at the revelation.

"At that stage of his life, yes. A conjurer to be exact,'' Hester replied.

"But I thought he was a doctor of physic.''

"No, never, though that is what he claims to be today. He was a magician, a conjurer—even a sleep-inducer of sorts—though that was a most risky business that had gotten him into trouble in the past when he lived on the Continent.''

Arthur sat rigidly on the ground next to Hester, spellbound by her story, the pieces of his own immediate past locking together for the first time in many months. Hester continued her tale, "When Roger Chillingworth came to town, with his clever act of legerdemain, he conjured my father—convinced him to become his associate. It was another one of my father's ill-fated decisions, but he accepted the offer and, henceforth, became the promoter of Roger Chillingworth's show. He was known as The Great Kursar in those days and he prided himself as being both a scholar and a magician—a conjurer who had studied the history of his art. It was not long before the two of them decided that there was more money to be made in music halls and public meeting places than in obscure village drinking houses. Since a move in that direction demanded more variety, I soon found myself a part of Roger's conjuring act— the young woman who assisted him silently on stage, handing him his equipment, but occasionally participating in his more elaborate feats of prestidigitation.

"Can you see me on the stage of some music hall, my arm disengaged and levitating above my body? Can you see Roger Chillingworth placing my hand over the flames of a candle, yet causing me to suffer no injury from the experience? Oh, he became a most remarkable magician, his fame spreading from village to village, his demand greatly enhanced by my father's excellent promotion.''

"You could hold your hand above the flames of a candle and not be burnt?'' Arthur asked her, the fragments of his past coming together with a remarkable sense of déjà vu.

"That and many other feats. All trickery of the old man's devising, I assure you. He was a most accomplished magician, though fooling country people was never that difficult.''

"What happened? Why did you marry him?" Arthur asked.

"That was my father's decision, of course. As the routine became more successful and we began to live more prosperously than at any time in years, Roger placed increasing demands upon my father. Probably it was a matter of greed, since even the modest fee my father earned as promoter soon became a rather substantial amount. Roger wanted to keep all the money for himself, even though I was paid nothing at all for my part in the show.

"In time, I became a kind of fulcrum, caught between the two of them. There were constant threats from Roger that Father was no longer necessary—that their relationship would end. My father counteracted by saying that I would no longer assist Roger in his show. They argued for months on end. Certainly, now that he had experienced this recent security, Father did not want to lose it; yet he did not know if he could trust Roger because of indications he had had about improper acts of the past.''

"But your father must have been the one who suggested that you be married to him," Arthur interjected.

"Yes, that is true. I do not know to this day what finally prompted that decision—a kind of reconciliation, I suppose—but we were married, after Father stressed the exigency of this arrangement, its necessity for our continued survival.'' She paused for a moment, then added, ''And I, as his obedient daughter, necessarily agreed.''

"When was that?" Arthur asked her.

"When I was eighteen. After about three years of our association with Roger Chillingworth. I am not certain what I expected of the marriage. I had been around music halls and public places long enough to observe a good bit of licentious activity, to be sure, but I believe I thought that that was something concerning other people. And, in fact, nothing really changed after we were married, except that I no longer slept in the room with my father in that string of inns we stayed in during our travels. One night, I moved out of my father's room and into Roger Chillingworth's, and that was all the difference that I could detect for many a day.

"I think the real effect was on my father, who seemed to have regretted the decision as soon as the marriage took place. His health began to deteriorate almost immediately, as if some vampire were sucking blood from his body. He wasted away, visibly altered in a matter of months. When the physical impairment began to affect his work, the rift with Roger developed anew, the two men hardly ever speaking to each other except about such matters concerning the promotion of the show.

"Finally, two matters occurred in rapid succession, precipitating our hasty removal from the public arena. The first of these was Father's death, which I had already long feared and worried about. It posed an immediate dilemma for me, since though legally bound to Roger Chillingworth by marriage, and totally dependent upon him for my livelihood, I knew that I no longer had to fulfill my father's request by remaining with him." Arthur looked directly at Hester Prynne, at the emblem on her breast. It seemed to bear no relation to the story she had been relating. He wondered for a moment if the *A* on her breast were not some part of Roger Chillingworth's conjuring act.

"For a few brief weeks after Father's funeral, we took a sojourn to Holland, visiting some of Roger's old friends. I thought that he had returned to his earlier scholarly pursuits and that perhaps I could even be happy with him. But then, shortly, we returned to the old way of life, and I knew I had to leave him. That proved to be unnecessary because of an unexpected event. Roger told me I did not need to appear with him on stage for a while. I do not think that this was an example of his concern for my troubled state, because of my father's recent death, but, rather, his way of informing me that I was totally dependent upon him, that he could perform without me, unassisted. It was a kind of warning, perhaps, that he did not need me, but that I needed him for my continued livelihood. The lesson struck home. As you can guess, Father had left me nothing.

"Then a few days later everything changed, and though I still do not understand all that happened in that terrible period of our lives, I know enough to put the story together. In my absence from the stage, Roger frequently called upon volunteers from the audience to assist him in his daring feats of conjury. And then one of his experiments failed, and the arm that he was supposedly severing from a volunteer and then magically restoring was badly injured."

Arthur gasped at Hester's story, a sense of relief passing through his mind for the first time as he realized that he was not the worst of Roger Chillingworth's victims.

"The boy, the volunteer, subsequently died. The device in the illusion that was supposed to engage the false blade did not function as it should. The blade had cut deeply into the boy's arm, even into the bone, and he later bled to death. Roger came running to our room, where we hurriedly packed our bags and fled the city where he had been presenting his routine.''

There were tears coursing down Hester's blanched face, and now that their roles as comforter had been reversed, Arthur grasped hold of Hester's hands and drew her toward him, smothering her against his own trembling breast. He held her tightly, not saying a word, until the paroxysms of her body had subdued and she was calm. When she began again, he was startled by her suggestion.

"We must move out of this secret retreat, Arthur. We must not stay hidden away like this any longer. All my life I have felt that I have had something to hide." She stood up and made an opening in the wall of shrubbery, and Arthur followed her to the edge of the brook where they sat down on the ground again, the sunshine darting all around them. In the distance, Pearl played quietly as though unaware of their more open existence.

"There is not much more to relate. I did not know what had happened until after we had fled the city where the accident occurred. He would not tell me. We took a carriage to Liverpool, and there Roger placed me on the ship for New England, under an assumed name, refusing to come with me until he had salvaged his assets spread throughout the country. He was to follow once these were collected. Everything had happened so quickly—my father's death, the accident, and then our new identities—I hardly knew what to do, except agree to board the ship. But once that ship set sail, I determined never to live with him again."

She stopped talking, as if she had reached the conclusion of her narrative.

"This is not at all the story I heard from Roger Chillingworth," Arthur responded, "yet I see now the manner in which he tried to trap me into relating incidents from my own private life. He did admit that he had been married, but the account of his marriage was entirely different."

"I am not surprised. He has always been a good storyteller."

"He said that his wife was Jewish, and he had saved her from a fate worse than death."

"That is not entirely incorrect. My mother was a Jewess, though I am not certain that my father ever revealed that fact to Roger Chillingworth."

"When was he supposed to leave the Old World to join you here?"

"I never knew for certain. My departure was so hasty that there was little time for plans such as that. All I knew was that he had said he intended to follow soon, after collecting whatever he could. Because we have never talked about these matters since his arrival here, I know little more than you. Whatever created the delay, only he himself knows."

"You have not spoken to him during all these years?" Arthur asked her.

"Only the day of my exposure upon the scaffold and now most recently when I asked him to cease his torturings of you."

"What did he respond? I almost fear to ask."

"That you were responsible for constructing your own prison, that he had done nothing except observe you as he would any patient who came to him for advice."

"Oh, Hester, he has perpetrated the most murderous tricks upon me—even inducing some kind of soporific state so I would reveal to him while I was under his control what I would never freely tell him otherwise. His devices for driving me mad have been as endless as these seven years. Lies, deceit, cunning tales of trickery about his months as captive among barbarous Indians in New-found-land."

"New-found-land?" Hester asked him, the expression on her face belying her surprise.

"Yes, New-found-land, where he claims to have been saved by a pocket watch with an alarm that frightened the savages. A family heirloom of some kind."

"That cannot be. There was never any such watch. He smashed the one he carried with him shortly after we were married—one day when I said something about his age. Henceforth, he refused to wear one."

"He claimed that he was tortured by Indians who forced him to carry live coals to light their tobacco."

Hester laughed. "That is another of his tricks from his years as a conjurer. Oh, there have clearly been no bounds to his cunning."

"You think he could not have been tortured?"

"That is difficult to believe, since a man of his age would find it difficult to survive the rigors of such an ordeal, though I do believe he has spent time living among the savages, somewhere to the south. That was the one fact he told me that afternoon in prison. When I asked him what he knew about medicine, he said he had lived with some peaceful Indians in the south, studying their medical lore."

"This is most confusing," Arthur replied. "He was never a doctor of physic in the old country?"

"Never, and that has been one of my constant fears. Not that his true profession would be discovered, but that by his limited knowledge of these remedies, he would do more harm to his patients than good. Imagine my bewilderment that afternoon when Master Brackett led him to my cell and introduced him as a doctor of physic."

"The rogue must be exposed. This concealment of his past has been as great as mine. I wonder at this ability to feign the knowledge of medicine."

"There is some basis for his current guise there. He was a student once, years ago, with the intent of becoming a physician. But some prank of his led to his dismissal from the university. I know little of his life before he joined with my father except for occasional remarks that slipped into his conversation. At one period in his life, he appears to have attempted experiments with alchemy and was forced to assume another identity after deceiving a great number of people. He never regarded himself as an entertainer as much as a scholar—of the black arts. He has studied much and read well, particularly in the possibilities of human duplicity. He made frequent reference to his days with Sir Thomas Overbury, as well as to aristocratic origins of his own and his apprenticeship to Doctor Forman, the famous conjurer, now dead. But he is no doctor of physic, that I assure you."

"If only you had told me these things seven years ago when Roger Chillingworth first entered my life—our lives. So much has changed since then, I do not even profess to understand what has happened."

"I did not know what to do. Before Pearl was born, I waited for some indication from you of what should be our future. But that sign was never made, and I assumed, for reasons best related to your ministry, there was nothing to be done and we would simply have to wait."

"It was my failure, Hester, to act in some decisive way. My life has been ruled for all this time by fear of the discovery of our crime, and—"

"It was no crime, Arthur. What we did had a sanctity of its own. No matter what pathway subsequent events took, I do not regret for one minute the conditions that first brought us together. Though I have worn this letter on my breast for seven long years, it has made no alteration in my personal feelings. Nothing has changed them and nothing will. It has been a symbolic gesture only, worn for other people around me." With her hand she undid the clasp that held the letter on her breast.

With wonderment in his eyes, Arthur watched as Hester threw the fateful symbol to her side. The removal had been so sudden he did not know what to expect other than awe that she was not struck down immediately by the hand of God. What courage Hester continued to demonstrate! If only his own troubles could be brushed aside so easily. She removed the cap that confined her luxuriant hair and let it cascade down her shoulders.

"Why have we waited so long for this moment, Arthur?" There was passion in her voice, and for a second Arthur felt that the past had been restored intact, whole, like some delicate object of blown glass that has survived an unexpected blow, as it had been so many years ago. He held her in his arms, thinking about the fragility of his earlier acts.

"I tried to send you some kind of message after Pearl's birth, some indication that we could meet here again and discuss our private lives," Arthur sadly replied. With his right hand he made a gesture at the grotto from which they had recently emerged. "I came here several times and once even removed the collar from my cassock and left it here, hoping that if you discovered it, you would understand my desire to communicate with you."

Hester grasped hold of his hand again, clenching it on the ground between them. "Oh, Arthur, had I only known. It was the one place to which I was afraid to return, the one symbol of our happiness I wanted to retain intact in my memory—sacred as the day we first set forth in it. I was afraid to seek you out in some other part of the forest, since Mistress Hibbins kept following me—especially during the months after my release from confinement."

A shadow of gloom passed over their heads. When he looked above them, Arthur discovered that a bank of white clouds had covered the sky, momentarily cutting off the earlier flood of sunshine. He thought about the revelations of the past hour, then asked Hester, futilely, "Whatever are we to do now, Hester? Will there never be escape from this fear that gnaws so steadily at my breast?"

"Not as long as you remain here, Arthur. Not as long as Roger Chillingworth can use you as the subject of his experiments. His is by far the greater evil. Though I have always known to expect the basest aspect of his character, never did I suspect that he would turn into such a fiend as this. His very figure is repugnant to me. I wonder how I endured this monster for so long a time. I have cursed the day our lives became entwined. Can you but forgive me for my error in not telling you of the man's true identity?''

"All is forgiven, Hester. And yet even knowing what I do now, I know not what move to make. I know not how to face this man. It will be all the more difficult once he sees me since he will determine immediately that we have spoken and that I know the nature of his true identity.''

"We must leave this place, Arthur, and start anew. It is what we should have done eight years ago, before my condition became publicly known.''

"We?'' Arthur asked, praying that he had heard Hester correctly.

"Yes, of course, we three. We must return to England, where we can re-create our lives as once we lived them. There is a ship in the harbor recently come from the Spanish Main on which we can certainly book passage and return full speed to the life that is rightly ours.''

Arthur trembled at the idea of such blessed relief, wondering if he dared permit himself to consider the possibility of a future free from agony. "When will that ship leave the port?'' he asked her, an image of the vessel at sea filling his consciousness. Could he dare place his hopes upon such simple matters?

"I do not know, but I will find out directly and make the necessary arrangements for the three of us.''

"Let us pray that it is soon, but not until I have delivered my Election Sermon. Though I await this freedom with renewed hope, I do not want to leave my people until I have delivered this final sermon.''

"Then we will begin again,'' Hester continued, "and you must learn to love and care for our child as I have.''

"I have often been afraid of children, Hester, and most especially of little Pearl—always fearful that people would detect my countenance in hers. I have loved her with the safety of a distance, afraid of a closer relationship.''

"You need not fear; she will come to love you also. She has been my one source of comfort these many years, my one true friend and confidante,'' and with that, Hester called into the distance and told Pearl to come and talk to the minister.

Arthur watched as the child advanced in their direction, her typical flighty movements slowed and measured—even the usual sparkle in her eyes altered to confusion and restraint. Was it possible that he was the source of this fear that had been engendered so suddenly in the child?

"Come quickly, Pearl," Hester exhorted. "The minister would talk with you. Do not be so slow."

But Pearl advanced only so far and then stopped in her tracks as if there were some kind of invisible barrier separating her from the two of them. Something was wrong, clearly making her afraid to walk any further, and Arthur could only conclude that his fear was matched by her doubt of him. How would the three of them ever live together as husband, wife, and child? He was about to whisper something to Hester, when she spoke again to the girl.

"Silly child, what troubles you?" her mother asked, clearly provoked by Pearl's unusual behavior. Then Arthur watched as Pearl pointed with her finger at the scarlet letter Hester had thrown upon the ground.

"How blind of me," Hester spoke aloud, reaching out and picking up the emblem from the grass. "Pearl has never seen me without this letter on my breast. It is me she shies away from, not you, Arthur." With that statement, she clasped the embroidered letter back upon her bosom and rolled her hair back within her cap.

"Do you recognize your mother now?" Hester asked the child. "Can you come here and meet the minister?" Pearl continued her advance, shortly standing in front of them. "Can you speak to the minister and welcome him as your spiritual father?" Hester asked their child.

"He is not my spiritual father," Pearl announced, as if speaking to a crowd of concerned onlookers. Arthur felt as if the invisible barrier had once again fallen between the two of them.

"But he loves you as your father, Pearl. And you must love him, too, for we will by and by see much of one another."

"Will we walk hand in hand in the village together?" Pearl asked her mother, without looking in Arthur's direction. "Will we stand on the public platform again in daylight instead of nighttime?"

"Surely in some future time, but not tomorrow. Come kiss the minister for we must soon away." Hester nudged the child in Arthur's direction but barely before he could embrace her, after the briefest touch, Pearl spun around and ran to the brook and washed off Arthur's embrace as if it had been of poison.

"Do not worry about Pearl," Hester admonished a few minutes later as they separated before leaving the forest. "The scarlet letter will leave no stain on her. Our child will never stumble where her parents fell."

Chapter Fourteen

Arthur left the forest a different man from the one who had entered it. Though he was disturbed that he had to leave separately from Hester and Pearl, that mother and daughter dared not return to the village at his side, his spirits had taken a decided upturn. His mind was still alive with the suggestions that Hester had proposed for their flight, though some much deeper instinct told him to act cautiously, to control his actions and his movements until after the Election Sermon, three days hence. Thus he wore, again, a kind of Janus mask: one minute smiling at the idea of their future life together, free from Roger Chillingworth's clutches; the next minute his countenance returning to his typical, more severe expression. In short, although he had entered the forest as one unified, though downtrodden, personality, he left it as two—each side of his character pulling at the other, threatening to destroy its counterpart.

To the villagers he passed on his way home—clogging the street with their late afternoon activities—he knew he appeared unchanged: the somber cleric they were accustomed to, who rarely smiled and usually held his hand over his breast. The ideas that flashed through his mind, however, triggered by the people he encountered, were far from consistent with those of his recent years. He yearned to dance over to one of the most devout crones of his parish and inform her that all life was nothing but sham, a distorting mirror, that even she in her extreme religiosity was living a life of concealed duplicity. What would she do if he told her these truths? It was all he could do to contain himself and refrain from running over to a group of schoolchildren who were chanting a pious rhyme and teach them the words to a dirty ditty he had learned as a child, forgotten for years, but now at this moment suddenly remembered. These thoughts that flashed through his mind took him totally by surprise.

Hester had released him from the horrible past, just as she had freed herself. Yet that glimmer of light for their future lives, that ray of hope, by necessity would remain no more than that—at least for several more days until she could work out the particulars of their flight from Boston after Arthur had delivered his parting sermon. But what were three or four days to the lifetime of mortification he would certainly lead if he remained a part of the Boston community? Turning down another lane, he permitted the slightest smile to cross his face. Fortunately, the street was empty; he was alone and no one would detect his expression.

When he reached the Widow Kellings's dwelling, his earlier trepidation began to return. The sun had disappeared over the housetops and though dusk was still an hour or so away, it would shortly be time for his evening repast—the meal he always shared with his landlady and Roger Chillingworth. Did he have the necessary strength to face the two of them? Was his newly discovered freedom to be destroyed this quickly? Till the very last moment of his life in Boston, was this monster of inhumanity going to control him like a puppet on a string? Somehow, the strings had all become entangled, but the puppeteer was still in charge, each step, each move, more restricted than before. Was Roger Chillingworth the price one paid for a life of sin and duplicity?

Hesitantly, he placed his hand on the doorlatch and turned it, pushing with his weight at the same time to move the mass of heavy oak inward. To his surprise, it swung with such ease that one would have thought a second person were pulling upon it at the same time, but no one was there. The room was empty, though Arthur could smell the aroma of the evening meal emanating from the kitchen at the back of the house. The Widow Kellings was probably out behind, overseeing the cook at her work. If he crossed the room quickly, he could retreat into his own chamber until dinner was ready and collect himself for the subsequent encounter with Roger Chillingworth.

His head tilted downward so he could look at the steps as he climbed them, Arthur bumped into old Roger Chillingworth who had suddenly materialized at the top of the staircase. Arthur tripped and the older man reached out and kept him from falling.

"What is the hurry, good Reverend Dimmesdale?" the leech asked as he helped support his younger ward.

"Nothing," Arthur replied, shaking off Chillingworth's hand and continuing on his way again to the safety of his room. "I was just returning," he added, his hand uncontrollably darting to his breast.

"One would think you were being chased by the Devil," Roger Chillingworth continued. "You look as white as a sheet. Here, let me assist you. I will give you some medicine to still your nerves," and he reached out to help Arthur walk down the hall to his room.

Arthur moved backward, determined not to let the older man touch him again. Already he felt as if he had been poisoned. "I am all right!" he replied emphatically, the forcefulness of his voice surprising him. "I simply tripped on the step." He pointed in the direction of the staircase, as if Roger Chillingworth could not be aware of its existence. "I am no longer in need of your remedies." And he quickly added, "I have told you this before. I do not need your assistance."

He turned his back on Roger Chillingworth, knowing that the older man had already detected the change in him, that the leech knew that Arthur had learned about his true character. He had been unable to conceal his bitterly acquired knowledge.

"One moment, good Reverend," Roger Chillingworth called down the hall after him. Though he wanted to enter his room without looking back, Arthur turned, obedient to the final moment. Roger Chillingworth continued: "Will you tell the widow that she need not set my place for supper?" Arthur was about to ask for an explanation when the older man provided one. "I must visit a patient in the country and will be gone at least until the morrow. Perhaps several days. Tell her that she need not set my place until I return."

Arthur nodded in reply, the earlier smile returning to his mouth. His image of Roger Chillingworth, at the opposite end of the hall, was that of a burning fire.

During the night, it was impossible for Arthur to sleep. His mind, suddenly unlocked of the fears that had tortured him for so many years, soared at the possibility of imminent release. What he expected would bring untroubled sleep had the opposite effect upon his consciousness. His heart beat faster; his mind reeled with a thousand images of the past and the Old World where he had grown up as a child, his mother's household, his older sisters, his student days at Oxford. He lay there tense in his bed, his body almost rigid. Every noise outside the window and inside the room reminded him of his temporality. He felt as if he had been shut away inside some kind of dark cavern. Even the sounds of his own breathing disturbed him, making it impossible to sleep.

Would Hester be able to book passage for them? Would it be possible to keep their flight from Boston a secret until the vessel was safe at sea? Would their lives in England bring the freedom for which his body and soul had yearned for so many years? What would they do for their means of livelihood once they returned to the old country? Would Pearl learn to love him or continue to fear him as she had in the past? He thought of the child during the afternoon, washing off his embrace in the brook. What did he know about children? Much less about conjugal love. What did he know about anything except for the narrow world of pain and fear he had carved for himself in the wilds of this heathen world?

He could not sleep. And yet there was work to be done if they were going to flee from Boston on that ship. The Election Sermon lay on his desk where it had been started the week before, a string of pious examples to provoke the minds of his parishioners without unduly disturbing them. Suddenly, what he had written, what he thought he had worked on so diligently, seemed quite unsuitable for the final colloquy with his followers. If he delivered what he had written, he would leave his people just as he had lived among them the past eight years: a total fraud, hidden in their midst. Was that the purpose of his religion—to offer a cloak to hide behind? Was he, Arthur Dimmesdale—the walking example of their orthodoxy—the true measure of God's duplicity?

He tried to pray. But the words that should have been automatic would not come to his lips. He climbed out of bed and knelt on the floor, but no prayer came to his muddled mind. The God he had prayed to, fought with, and secretly denied for eight hypocritical years had become distant, was even scorning him, refusing to listen to his urgent pleas. With his knees on the hardwood floor and his hands on the edge of the bed, he moved his head up and down, knocking his forehead against the board at the side of the straw-ticked mattress. Was this the culmination of all these years of infamy? Would God provide no clue at all concerning the pathway he should follow in the future?

The logic of Hester's proposal began to collapse. How could they flee to England without being subsequently discovered? Was there any place on this earth where they could move to and keep their horrible secret from publicly exploding? Would the fear of discovery continue to control their very lives, even after they returned to the old country? Was it possible to hide their secret from God? As he banged his head against the bed, he knew that Hester's suggestion was a futile one. It had a hollow ring to it like a cracked bell-glass. There was no way to hide from God or his minions on this earth. There was no reason to flee to the Old World unless the flight were preceded by a public confession, releasing him of his terrible burden. Without the willful exposure of his secret past, the new life in England would be haunted by the same inner furies that had dominated his life for this unending string of years.

If he delivered the Election Sermon as it had been written, it would simply be another stage down the path of mendacity. The persona he had created to harangue his followers would dominate his existence until the end. Lies and deceit, from this man of little faith who walked the streets amongst them—who dared to step into the pulpit of First Church several times each week and mock them with his guile. Their revered pastor was the biggest fraud of all— the cracked symbol of holiness, wrongly honored and emulated. Surely he had made a pact with the Devil himself, or all religion was nothing more than a fraud for the masses.

He raised himself from the floor, rubbing his forehead with his hands. The pain shot through his skull, but he was not certain if it was the result of the movements against the board or the internal agony that refused to go away. He crossed his room, lit a candle with the flintlock, and examined the pages of the Election Sermon. Then, a moment later, he tore them into shreds and threw them into the empty fireplace. He would start all over again. There would be no reason for leaving with Hester and Pearl if first he did not publicly confess his sins and transgressions.

Barely had he reached his decision to open his heart when he was assailed by fresh doubts. If he confessed his secret crimes, if he bared his breast for all to see, would not the result be so overpowering, so debasing that it would be almost the same as if he had not? The agony of release would be followed by immediate humiliation, by such wretched agony that no support he could gain even from Hester and the child would be capable of lifting him out of the mire of public exposure. When the three of them left on the ship after his public confession, their crime would follow them to the end of the world. Who would even consent to marry them once their villainy became publicly known? How could they live as man and wife? What difference at all would his confession make for their future lives?

He paced his room—the once familiar environment no longer the source of warmth and comfort it had been. His sin was so great that it was irrevocable. There was no escape. If he climbed the steps of the pulpit and shouted out his malefaction, his secret pollution of the church would be made public and everyone would feel defiled by his revelation. The church would need to be ritualistically sanctified. He would die from public humiliation. It was impossible for him to confess, since their flight to the old country would be meaningless without purgation.

At six o'clock in the morning—exhausted from his inner battle—he returned to his bed and fell into a deep slumber.

When he awoke, he was struck by an inner peace that had come to his soul. He felt calm and refreshed as if he had slept for many, many hours. Bright motes of sunlight shot through the flaxen curtains of his room; outside he knew it was a beautiful day. He climbed out of bed, not even bothering to rub his eyes. When he pulled back one of the curtains, the room was bathed in the fresh morning sunlight, and he blinked several times in order to adjust his eyes before he placed his glasses on his face. Outside the sky had taken on the appearance of a perfect heron blue; there was not a cloud to be seen on the horizon over the cemetery. He leaned on the windowsill for a moment and took in the spectacular beauty of the day. The air was fresh and calm; he could feel the warmth of the summer morning rushing into the room and was struck by the totality of the silence from the outer world. The universe had been altered around him; the hush of stillness contributed to his inner tranquillity.

Quickly, he pulled off his sleeping garment, startled by the unexpected move. He stood there utterly naked, examining his body, unafraid to glance at the forbidden areas, the stark white flesh, surprised that no profane thought entered his mind. The letter on his chest had disappeared. His body no longer repelled him. He was not afraid of his total nakedness, of the severe brightness of the daylight reflecting upon it. Adjusting slowly to this amazing change, he crossed the room to his dresser and removed the clothing he would wear for the day: fresh undergarments, clean stockings and a handkerchief, an ironed collar for his cassock. When he had finished dressing, he left his room to complete his morning toilet.

Refreshed by these activities, he walked down the staircase and into the sitting room of the Widow Kellings's house. Somewhere in the distance—in the kitchen, no doubt—he could hear the widow puttering around, helping prepare the morning meal. Arthur called out a good-day to her and then looked around the room, absolutely glowing from the beauty of the morning outside. There were fresh-cut flowers on the dining table, the room itself was spotless, the whitewashed walls so immaculate in the spectacular brightness that they looked as if they had been repainted during the night. His eye took in once familiar objects he had completely forgotten, his mind for so long directed only upon himself and his own inner turmoil. Nothing was changed in the room from the way it had always been, from the hundreds of days he had come and gone, from the thousands of meals he had eaten there. Yet everything was different, fresher, newer—as if every object in the chamber had been replaced by a perfect replica of its original, unmarked by the scourges of time and habitude.

When the Widow Kellings entered the room, followed by the servant holding two plates of overflowing food for their morning repast, Arthur thought that even she was different from the way he had always remembered her. "Good morning, Reverend," she said cheerfully. "What a beautiful day it is." The servant placed the plates of hot food on the previously set table and the two of them sat down.

"Is Roger Chillingworth still away?" Arthur asked her, after agreeing with her statement about the harmony of the day.

"I have not seen him since yesterday," the widow replied, and then they bent their heads and paused a moment for silent prayer before breakfast.

When he looked up again, he was struck by the widow's own beauty. She looked more radiant than he could ever recall. Her hair, which had been gray and always knotted in a bun, hung loosely around her face and was darker than he remembered—almost chestnut—and Arthur wondered if the brightness of the morning sun had something to do with it.

They chatted in a friendly manner about nothing significant, all the while Arthur feeling more relaxed at the table than he had in months. He had come to dread these meals shared with Roger Chillingworth, and breakfast was always the worst since the widow usually left the two of them to pursue their own topics of conversation.

When he arose from the table at the end of the meal and caught a final glance of the Widow Kellings, he thought she looked twenty-five years younger. The wrinkles he had remembered on her face were gone, and even her physical movements were more sprightly than he could recollect. As she disappeared into the kitchen, Arthur blinked his eyes a couple of times, aware again of the translucence of the day.

He was about to return to his room to work on the Election Sermon when he heard voices coming from Roger Chillingworth's room. Confused, since he believed that the leech was still visiting a patient in the country, he walked down the hall and looked through the old man's open door, carefully so that he would not be detected. To his wonder, there was Roger Chillingworth, talking rapidly to some younger gentleman dressed in such finery as Arthur had rarely seen in all of New England. The younger man was sitting in a chair with his back turned toward him, making it impossible for Arthur to see if he could recognize him.

As for the leech himself, he stood near the fireplace. Though it was a summer day, flames were coming from the hearth, and Arthur could see a kettle on a tripod, boiling above the whitehot lambent flames. He thought he smelled sulphur or some other substance that was inside the cauldron. What further confused him was the physical appearance of Hester's husband, for he, too, looked much younger than Arthur had ever remembered. His body was less stooped, the hair on his head more plentiful—in every way Arthur knew that he was looking at a younger man.

"How long will the experiment take?" the figure in the chair asked in an excited, almost feminine voice.

"That is difficult to say, since the alloys employed must be heated until they attain their proper mixture. Sometimes a day, sometimes longer," the rogue replied.

"You mean that it will not be this afternoon? My gold will take longer than that?" the younger man questioned, the pitch of his voice belying his troubled concern.

"Tomorrow perhaps, or the day after more likely, but I will need to purchase some additional supplies for which you must reimburse me, or, if you are prepared at this time, what greater convenience for us than now?"

It appeared as if the gentleman in the chair were about to reach into some purse concealed on his person. Arthur considered entering the room and warning the gentleman of Roger Chillingworth's trickery, but did not remain to witness the final tableaux of the act. He turned around and glanced down the hall at the open door to his room, the rays of the sunshine bursting forth even there and dancing lightly on the polished floor.

"Is this the way death will be?" he asked himself in a hushed voice, as he stood silently in the hall for a second before returning to his own room. The stillness was once again overpowering. There was no longer the sound of voices coming from Roger Chillingworth's room or any sign of movement in the rest of the house. Once again he was struck by the tranquillity of the universe, and he realized that no sounds were coming from the outside world. The usual hum of insects, of birds chirrupping, of leaves stirring—none of these sounds were audible to his ears. Obviously the explanation was that he was standing in the hallway of the widow's house, a distance from any open windows. He stood there for another moment trying to decide what move to make. It was a simple matter. All he needed to do was to stand at one of the windows in his room and listen. He walked down the passage to the open door and was about to enter it, when he discovered that someone else was already inside.

Because of the brightness of the morning sun, it was impossible to immediately recognize the figure in his room. Arthur leaned against the doorjamb and blinked his eyes several times in rapid succession. His confusion lasted for only a minute or two and then he identified this bold figure who was sitting in one of the chairs near a window, reading a leather-bound book, unconcerned about his presence in the door. Arthur knew that he was looking at himself. It was a disturbing feeling, for the figure in the chair was much younger than he—still an adolescent—innocent of the ravages of time. His head was tilted slightly to one side, his face—even at that angle—revealed a sense of inner peace and serenity. Arthur watched him turn a page of the volume he held in his left hand, utterly engrossed in his reading. As the page was turned, it was possible to see a cat, which the boy was stroking with his hand, asleep in his lap. On the floor near the side of the chair were a pair of crutches.

Arthur moved back away from the doorjamb, wondering if he dared disturb the boy from his reading. He felt an almost uncontrollable desire to speak to his younger self, to communicate some subtle warning to this free spirit not yet disillusioned by the realities of maturity, but he was not certain how to begin such a conversation. He looked away from the boy at the rest of the room for just a moment, wondering if it too was altered in any manner from the way he had remembered it. Then he heard the youth's laughter, and the urge to walk over to him and embrace his younger self was so powerful that he passed under the lintel and rushed across the room, as the vision disappeared before his eyes. In his confusion, in the ache of his disappointment, he reached out and touched the empty chair. The upholstery was still warm, and there was an indentation in the cushion where the boy had been seated.

An overwhelming sense of sadness engulfed Arthur—the futility of having missed some momentous event in his life—but a moment later he was stunned by joy. He stood near the empty chair, in the stillness of the bright sun, an empty vessel, yet one that had known utter fullness. He thought of Hester and then of Pearl—lovingly, caringly, paternally. Then he raised his head and looked outside at the brightness of the summer day. Nothing had changed from the way it had been when he had first awakened: the sky retained its royal blue sharpness, the sun shone with an intensity he had never before experienced, there was a total finality of silence in the universe. Though the casement was open, no sound from the outside world entered the chamber. The remainder of the house was silent.

Exactly how long he stood there, looking out the window, he did not know. It might have been hours; it may have been only a matter of a few minutes. Time itself had become irrelevant. It no longer mattered. When the sun crossed his angle of vision, turning everything into a pale, pink whiteness, he kept his eyes transfixed upon the ocher sphere, knowing that he would be blinded by the intense fire but that the outer darkness would be transformed into inward light. He removed his glasses and stared at the sun until it sank over the edge of the horizon. Then he lowered himself to his knees, leaning his head on the windowsill in front of him, and prayed—not to the God of wrath he had fought against for eight terrible years, but to the God of love he felt infused within his inner breast.

Chapter Fifteen

Looking away from the procession in front of him—at the throng of people in the marketplace—Arthur permitted himself a hurried glance into the crowd in search of Hester and their child. In a matter of minutes, the serpentine column would wind itself into the church and it would be impossible to identify them, since he knew that mother and child would not enter the holy structure during such a momentous occasion as the inauguration of the new governor. Because it was the Election Sermon he was about to deliver, Arthur guessed that he was being watched by a thousand eyes, that his public demeanor by necessity should mirror the stateliness of the occasion. As the procession marched slowly forward, he refrained from glancing around at the mass of people in the square and exchanging any sign of recognition with his villagers. Yet he wanted to capture one fleeting image of Hester Prynne before he entered the church in order to locate her position outside.

His appearance to all who observed him was certainly that of a creature more otherworldly than worldly. As he trailed the line of figures in front of him (the musical accompaniment followed by the personages of authority and exemplars of the state, the magistrates and lesser functionaries), he felt almost as if he were floating above the ground, so little an affect did this display of symbolic magnificence have upon him. His mind was, rather, upon the sermon itself, his confession and his hard-earned escape from temporality. His head was held high, his eyes affixed on the backs of the figures in front of him, though even in that rigidly official position it was possible to scrutinize the people in the gathering if he moved his eyes to the periphery. There were, in fact, more people in the market on this public holiday than he could remember from previous such occasions: the usual mixture of citizens and assorted riffraff from the village and the neighboring environs, a goodly number of friendly Indians, and here and there a knot of sailors from the ship on which Hester had said she would book their passage.

Arthur had observed all this out of the corner of his eye, without having to move his head and destroy the image of solemnity he had established by his stance. As the procession circled around the edges of the market, he knew the place where he should search for Hester, though they had not discussed her appearance at the public event. He thought he could identify voices from the crowd, and recognized here and there the visage of some member of his parish, some friend of his years of toil in the New World. Walking immediately in front of him was the Reverend John Wilson, senescent and more hesitant of step than in years of yore, but still the venerable figure he had always appeared to be to these coarsely dressed Puritans of the wild. As Arthur walked past the base of the scaffold where he had determined that Hester and Pearl would be standing, he permitted himself that singular glance away from the figures in front of him and identified mother and child isolated slightly from the rest of the denizens, standing inside an invisible circle.

This was all that he needed—the assurance that Hester was waiting at the base of the scaffold, the symbolic structure where their public ignominy had begun and where it would shortly end. His lips moved ever so slightly in a sign of recognition so that Hester would realize that he had observed her there, though he was afraid that she might misconstrue the meaning of his glance. Then his eyes refocused upon John Wilson's back, upon his spiritual mentor's black cassock adorned with white lace and ermine. The sound of the musical instruments from the head of the procession was suddenly diminished by the musicians' entry into the church, yet Arthur kept his step, following the unseen leader of these earthly mortals on this final day of recognition and public exposure of his own secret life.

The moment for the delivery of his sermon arrived. Arthur left his chair on the dais and climbed the steps to the pulpit like one in a trance—yet a proud, determined figure aware of his limited sojourn on this planet. He looked at the sea of faces before him, the greater and the lesser functionaries of the Boston community, identifying the one fateful blemish in the crowd. He announced the topic of his sermon—the moieties of New England and their sacred reiationship with the Deity—and then began delivering his lengthy discourse, elaborating as he developed his theme, illustrating the thesis and the antithesis by the use of several carefully chosen Biblical examples. At length, he came to the final exemplary tale with which he wanted to conclude his sermon, taken intentionally from the secular instead of the sacred:

"In the not too distant past, a young man named Ulrich Zimmer arrived one day at Frankfort on the Main with the intention of completing his studies for a degree in medicine. He was an astute and earnest student, rarely given to the more common abuses of the body or the mind. His family could rest assured that he would work diligently and one day bring honor to their name.

"At the university, Ulrich's studies advanced satisfactorily until some months after his arrival when he fell in love with the daughter of one of his professors. This young woman, whose name was Helen, was the only child of the revered scholar, Michael Furst, regarded by his students as a tyrant and a continuing obstruction to the completion of their studies. More than one young medical student had left the university disgraced, failing to achieve the level of excellence demanded by Professor Furst's impossible goals. More than one student had fallen in love with the professor's beautiful but unattainable daughter and had left the university in a state of emotional collapse.

"Through the years many of them had watched Helen assist her father in his experiments, the beauty of this creature in sharp contrast to the gnarled and aged body of her overly protective father. Some students doubted that the old man could be her legitimate sire. In time, an intense feeling of animosity developed between Professor Furst and his students because of the way he displayed his daughter in front of them—like some expensive but untouchable prize, always reminding them of the power he held over their studies. Helen was, in fact, her father's sole companion, her mother having died when she was still a child. Professor Furst raised her with his overbearing nature, loving her with such deep emotion that several of his colleagues had suggested an unnatural relationship between them.

"In a way, Ulrich was only the last in a series of young men who had become enchanted by the distant and unattainable Helen. What came to distinguish him from his predecessors was his determination to meet with her secretly and bare his heart to her, a goal that had never been achieved by any of the other young men in Professor Furst's classes. What was equally remarkable was Ulrich's discovery that the only time Helen was unattended was when the professor convened with his colleagues at the university. It was during one of those meetings when Ulrich found the time to declare his love for Helen.

"To his surprise and delight, the young woman returned his affection—her own nascent feelings only partially repressed by her domineering father. She had longed for such a man as Ulrich, just as he had yearned for her. Their secret meetings shortly became Helen's entire life, as these young lovers plotted their way of escaping the old man's control.

"Unbeknownst to the young lovers, Professor Furst suspected that his daughter was being removed from his sphere of influence by one of his students, but he was unable to determine the youth's identity. Clever rogue that he was, he instigated a series of experiments upon her—an artificial form of somnambulism—permitting him to talk to Helen while she was in a sleeplike trance, so she would reveal information she would never have told him during her normal lucid state. It was in such a manner that Doctor Furst was able to learn about Helen's secret encounters and intended elopement with Ulrich Zimmer.

" 'You have ruined our family name and violated a sacred trust!' he screamed at his daughter a day or so later, attempting to convince Helen that he had learned about her relationship with Ulrich from one of his colleagues and not through the violation of her secret thoughts. 'This young Zimmer will leave the university and you will never see him again!'

" 'I have done nothing of which you or I should be ashamed,' Helen replied, asserting for the first time her stronger self. 'We will be married—either with your blessing or without.'

" 'Can you leave your poor father as easily as that?' Furst asked her, appealing to the emotions that had kept her in his control for so many years. 'Would you renounce your life and all that I have taught you for someone as common as this?'

"Though she was nearly swayed from her love for Ulrich, Helen remained adamant, determined to end the stifling relationship with her father. After the dismissal of the young man from the university, she fled to the village of his family, seeking refuge and a new life with him there. Shortly, they were married—with the blessing of Ulrich's family—and they settled down to a life of happiness and contentment, Helen determining never again to communicate with her father.

"Close to a year later, when Helen was expecting their first child, her father appeared in their midst—his physiognomy even more infirm than before, the result of sudden blindness brought about during one of his experiments when the student assisting him had picked up the wrong chemical and added it to a beaker of boiling nitrate. The vapors from the admixture had arisen with such quickness that Professor Furst had been unable to move away. His eyesight, which had been perfect before, was reduced to total blindness.

"Even in this newly altered state of her father's dependence, Helen wanted nothing to do with him. She argued with Ulrich that they had no responsibility to take care of the old man. Ulrich, however, suffering from feelings of guilt because of his revered professor's blindness, convinced Helen that it was their moral duty to help the old gentleman in what would certainly be his declining years.

" 'I do not trust him even now,' Helen told Ulrich. 'Why must he live with us instead of some other place where we can make such arrangements for him as are necessary?'

" 'Children cannot treat their elders so casually,' Ulrich replied. 'This will lead to accusations of unnatural feelings for my own parents. What will they believe if we turn your father away?'

"In short, Ulrich convinced Helen that her father should live with them. The old man's previous attempts to thwart their marriage had nothing to do with his present needs. Christian charity demanded this simple gesture. So Professor Furst moved in with the couple, shortly before the birth of their child, and almost immediately their relationship took a change for the worse, the disruption of their marriage becoming as complete as Helen had feared.

"Old Furst knew that his hold on his daughter would never be the same as it had been before her marriage, so he worked on Ulrich, eating away at his soul, sucking his blood like a leech, determining that if he no longer had his daughter's love, no one else would have it either. In time, his control of Ulrich was complete. The younger man answered his father-in-law's every call, waited on him hand and foot, almost became his personal servant—all because of Furst's insinuations that the accident that resulted in his blindness would never have occurred if Ulrich had not stolen Helen away from him.

"It was not long after the birth of their child, a girl, that the love that Ulrich had for Helen moved from the marriage bed to the parlor, where the child and grandfather began to control his every move. Old Furst crippled Ulrich's love for his own child, for when the baby did not keep him awake at night, his father-in-law prevented him from sleeping in the day. Often the old man would awaken Ulrich to ask him the time of day, his empty eyes unable to distinguish light from darkness. The old man appeared to have developed an abnormal concern with the passing of time, as if his blindness had already made him a resident of that other world.

"One day, when he was passing the shops in the village where they lived, Ulrich noticed in one of the windows a clock that appeared to have numbers embossed upon its face. Immediately he thought of his father-in-law; this clock would permit the old man to set the alarm and determine the time by touch. Ulrich purchased the unusual object and presented it to his father-in-law, praying he had solved the problem of the old man's obsession with time.

"But nothing was changed. The old man ate away at Ulrich's heart, creating an even greater chasm between husband and wife. The child grew up a stranger to her father. As the years passed by, Ulrich's health began to deteriorate so rapidly that Helen came to fear that her husband's life would cease before her father's. One day she decided she must talk to her father about Ulrich's declining health.

"'You were once a doctor yourself. Is there nothing you can do for him?' she asked, when Ulrich was away.

"'How can I study the patient when I cannot even see him?' her father replied, staring blankly into space.

"'If you refuse, then I will take Ulrich to Frankfort where there are still colleagues of yours who will remember me. They will examine him and offer their analysis of this cancer that daily eats away at him.'

"'But there are doctors even here,' the old man replied, 'who can offer you the same kind of treatment.'

"'It is not the same, since their training has not been in these areas.' Helen thought she saw her father cringe. During the ensuing days when she made the necessary preparations for their trip, the old man's health began to waste away as if he were suddenly the patient in need of medical care. But she convinced Ulrich of the necessity of their sojourn; the child could remain for a few days with his parents. Her father would be cared for by the servants.

"As she had feared, the doctors in Frankfort were unable to determine a cause for Ulrich's troubled state, though they examined him with all the skill of their combined knowledge. The illness that gnawed away at his life appeared to have no origin within his body.

Ulrich would have returned to their home as he had left except for Helen's accidental revelation before they left the city.

"'What was the cause of my father's blindness?' she inquired of one of his elderly colleagues.

"'Of what blindness do you refer? Has Professor Furst lost his eyesight?' the man replied.

"'Was he not blind when he left the university?' Helen asked, determined to seek out an explanation for this inconsistency. 'Was there not an accident in the laboratory before he left?'

"'You jest. I myself was with him at the time of his departure, and there was nothing wrong with his eyesight.'

"The knowledge of this deceit was the cure that Ulrich needed. For seven long years this fiend who had lived with them had feigned blindness in order to spy upon them secretly and drive them insane with guilt. Ulrich was struck by his own shortsightedness, and Helen feared even more for his immediate safety.

"With their painful knowledge, they returned home but no longer to the joyous household they had known during the first months of their marriage. Old Furst, who knew immediately what they had discovered in Frankfort, wasted away as the days quickly passed, dying a few months later, his fraudulently empty eyes staring off into space. Ulrich's suffering remained as it was, and he accepted this as the common lot of men. Only Helen—who had understood the problem from the beginning—appeared to have learned something from the experience and determined that when their daughter grew to womanhood she would learn from the lesson of their sorrow."

Chapter Sixteen

Even before he left the pulpit, Arthur determined by the expressions on the faces of the people in the church that his sermon had been a failure. After the prayer that had followed his sermon, there was a kind of stunned silence from the overflowing crowd of people as if they were not certain whether their minister had finished or not. Arthur stood there immobile for a few seconds, searching their faces for some sign of recognition, waiting for something to happen. If his Election Sermon had been misunderstood, all the more reason for his public confession on the scaffold to clarify the abstruseness of his discourse. After the benediction, the musicians began their accompaniment for the recession as if signaled by the hand of some imperceptible force. When he turned and descended the steps from the pulpit, Arthur thought that tears had streaked the Reverend Wilson's hoary face, though in the light refracted within the church it was difficult to tell. Then the octogenarian turned his back toward him so that Arthur could follow him down the central aisle of the church.

As the recessional began, Arthur tried to locate Roger Chillingworth in the crowd of restless people, but the leech had apparently made a hasty exit from the church. For a moment, Arthur wondered if his tormentor hadn't simply shriveled up and blown away like a particle of ash. But, no, that could not be possible until he himself had vanished from the scene of their battleground. The faces of his parishioners became little more than a hurried blur as Arthur fled past them, though here and there he detected a muffled comment from one of his followers: "What was the purpose of his lengthy tale?" "Methinks his sermons are becoming more obscure.'' He even thought he heard one old crone mumble something about his days on earth being numbered, and he had to force himself not to smile openly at the remark.

Outside, the pace of the recession increased, and for a minute Arthur feared that he would lose his step. He had to act quickly now or the moment would be lost. There could be no turning back, either upon the horror of the past, so painfully clarified, or upon the falseness of their future life in the old country. The escape—if it was going to be achieved at all—was imminently desired, ardently wished for. He was going to take the burden upon his shoulders and stand before them, naked in the alliance of his flesh with all living matter. He breathed deeply, as if to pull together all his inner resources for this final demonstration of wholeness. The shackle that had harnessed him so tightly these several years slipped away like a yoke being lifted from some beast of burden, liberated and free of suffering at the hand of some benighted master.

The train of civic figures marched haughtily along the parameters of the village square, each individual majestically secure within his own private world, yet each personage subvening from the new governor that portion of his munificence as the public occasion demanded. No longer keeping his eyes affixed on the marchers in front of him, or upon old Reverend Wilson in particular, Arthur glanced quickly from visage to visage in the thickened crowd for the two familiar expressions which would assist him in his liberation. At a distance of some twenty feet or so from the scaffold, he began to feel faint, as if the courage he had mustered from his inner resources had unexpectedly snapped; but then the faces of the crowd propelled him onward and he saw Hester and Pearl, still—even within the ravenous force of the multitude—distanced and alone.

''Come hither, Hester—and little Pearl,'' he said to them, startled by the power of his voice.

The child danced over to him, the expression on her face ecstatically that of love. He had fulfilled her singular desire, publicly acknowledging her in the midst of the village square—instead of in the hidden recesses of the forest or of the night. She clasped her arms around his midriff, the warmth from her wrenlike body astonishing him and immediately enclosing him within a sheltered orb of abiding protection. Arthur placed his arms around her and lifted her up into the air, as her fantastic shrieks pierced the throng of confused villagers milling round about them. In an instant, she locked her hand firmly inside of his and they walked toward Hester—all these events materializing so quickly that the recession had scarcely missed a beat.

Then, with a suddenness matched only by Pearl's surprising flight into his arms, a dark shadow fell around them, as if the day of wrath had burst forth, opening up the ground and ejecting a hurricane of devils. Old Roger Chillingworth thrust himself into their midst, exploding with such force that Arthur felt he would be pushed over and trampled by the frenetic and unruly crowd. Arthur thought he saw Reverend Wilson and Governor Bellingham trying to come to his rescue. Arthur's glasses were knocked from his face and crushed into the ground.

"Madman! Do you think that you can escape so easily? Do you not believe that I will chase you to the ends of the world?"

"You cannot follow where I intend to go!" Arthur retorted. He shook the leech off with such ease that one would have thought he were freeing himself from but a few droplets of rain. Then he held his free hand out to Hester Prynne, the other still encircling the child's.

"Come, woman. It is but a few steps further, but all the difference on the pathway toward deliverance."

The crowd stirred as if some unconstrained force were swirling it around inside a gigantic churn. Every eye was focused upon Arthur Dimmesdale and his two wondrous companions. As Arthur led them to the bottom of the scaffold and began the ascent to the top, supported by Hester and the child but then in turn aiding them with his own renewed strength, he felt as if he were being lifted up into the firmament, floating—as in his dreams—above all earthly matters and consternations. Behind them, from the corner of his eye, he could see the black veil of their past, following like some obedient cur, humiliated yet bound to them by some invisible collar around his neck. He was surprised that the loss of his glasses did not impede his sight; his sense of rarified clarity was sharper than he could ever recall.

They slowly climbed the steps, the chain of love connecting them, each to the other two, passing through their hands by some impenetrable source of human kindness. There was no trembling within his body as there had been before, no sense of duty or obligation fraught with unresolved turmoil—only a great light that appeared to be coming toward them from some omnipotent source overhead. When they reached the final step and moved to the convergence of the platform, Pearl kissed him on the lips and Arthur knew that from that momentary blessing he was released forever from the temporality of his pain. He glanced above the multitude of faces, his eyes staring at the terra cotta sun, his blindness dissolved in the light of inner peace.

NEW FROM  AVON BARD

DISTINGUISHED MODERN FICTION

SENT FOR YOU YESTERDAY
John Edgar Wideman   82644-5/$3.50
In SENT FOR YOU YESTERDAY, John Edgar Wideman, "one of America's premier writers of fiction" (*The New York Times*), tells the passion of ordinary lives, the contradictions, perils, pain and love which are the blood and bone of everybody's America. "Perhaps the most gifted black novelist in his generation." *The Nation*

Also from Avon Bard: **DAMBALLAH** (78519-6/$2.95) and
HIDING PLACE (78501-3/$2.95)

THE LEOPARD'S TOOTH
William Kotzwinkle   62869-4/$2.95
A supernatural tale of a turn-of-the-century archaeological expedition to Africa and the members' breathtaking adventures with the forces of good and evil, by "one of today's most inventive writers." (Playboy).

DREAM CHILDREN
Gail Godwin   62406-0/$3.50
Gail Godwin, the bestselling author of A MOTHER AND TWO DAUGHTERS (61598-3/$3.95), presents piercing, moving, beautifully wrought fiction about women possessed of imagination, fantasy, vision and obsession who live within the labyrinths of their minds. "Godwin is a writer of enormous intelligence, wit and compassion...DREAM CHILDREN is a fine place to start catching up with an extraordinary writer." *Saturday Review*

NEW FROM ▟⌐ AVON BARD

DISTINGUISHED MODERN FICTION

THE VILLA GOLITSYN
Piers Paul Read   61929-6/$3.50
In this taut suspense novel by bestselling and award-winning author Piers Paul Read, an Englishman asked to spy on an old friend uncovers a shocking truth leading to death at a luxurious, secluded villa in southern France. "Substantial and vivid...The sexual intrigue reaches a high pitch." *The New York Times*

BENEFITS: A NOVEL
Zöe Fairbairns   63164-4/$2.95
Published in Great Britain to critical acclaim, this chilling futuristic novel details the rise to power in a future England of the "Family" party, which claims to cure the economic and social problems by controlling reproduction and institutionalizing motherhood. "A successful and upsetting novel." *The London Sunday Times* "Chilling Orwellian vision of society...an intelligent and energetic book." *The London Observer*

TREASURES ON EARTH
Carter Wilson   63305-1/$3.95
In 1911, a young photographer joins a Yale expedition to the Andes in search of a lost Incan city. In the midst of a spectacular scientific find—Machu Picchu—he makes a more personal discovery and finds the joy of forbidden love which frees his heart and changes his life. "Its power is so great, we may be witnessing the birth of a classic." *Boston Globe* "A fine new novel...beautifully and delicately presented." *Publishers Weekly*

NEW FROM AVON ⬧ BARD
DISTINGUISHED
MODERN FICTION

DR. RAT   63990-4/$3.95
William Kotzwinkle
This chilling fable by the bestselling author of THE FAN MAN
and FATA MORGANA is an unforgettable indictment of man's
inhumanity to man, and to all living things. With macabre
humor and bitter irony, Kotzwinkle uses Dr. Rat as mankind's
apologist in an animal experimentation laboratory gro-
tesquely similar to a Nazi concentration camp.

ON THE WAY HOME   63131-8/$3.50
Robert Bausch
This is the powerful, deeply personal story of a man who came
home from Vietnam and what happened to his family.
"A strong, spare, sad and beautiful novel, exactly what
Hemingway should write, I think, if he'd lived through the
kind of war we make now."   John Gardner
"A brilliant psychological study of an intelligent, close
family in which something has gone terribly and irre-
trievably wrong."   *San Francisco Chronicle*

AGAINST THE STREAM   63693-X/$4.95
James Hanley
"James Hanley is a most remarkable writer....Beneath this
book's calm flow there is such devastating emotion."
The New York Times Book Review
This is the haunting, illuminating novel of a young child
whose arrival at the isolated stone mansion of his mother's
family unleashes their hidden emotions and forces him to
make a devastating choice.